Kate felt hot tears start. . . .

"When were you going to tell me your boat was ready to sail?" Kate demanded. "As you waved good-bye on your way to Tahiti?"

Justin gripped her arms in his strong, callused hands. "I don't want to wave good-bye to you at all, Kate. I want you standing beside me. And I want you with me on the beach in Tahiti, or wherever. You know that."

Kate felt herself melting toward him. His touch had never failed to weaken her. But she shook her head. "Justin, you know that isn't going to happen."

"I don't know anything," Justin said stubbornly.

"You don't believe me, do you?" Kate asked. "In your heart, you think I'll end up going along."

Justin stopped and turned back toward her. "In my heart I believe you love me, and I love you."

"That doesn't mean I'll trade my dreams for yours," Kate said.

"They could be *our* dreams, Kate." Justin smiled sadly. "I know there's room in my boat for you. But your dreams . . . they've never included me."

He pushed past her. Kate felt hot tears start and was suddenly glad for her dark sunglasses.

Look for the other titles in the
Ocean City series

Ocean City
Love Shack
Fireworks

And don't miss
Freshman Dorm—the Hit Series!
by Linda A. Cooney

Now thirty-one titles strong!

And *Freshman Dorm Supers #1–#3*
Super-sized for extra fun!

BOARDWALK

Katherine Applegate

HarperPaperbacks
A Division of HarperCollins*Publishers*

For Leslie Morgenstein, Ann Brashares,
and the rest of the DWAI gang.
And, as always, for Michael.

HarperPaperbacks *A Division of* HarperCollins*Publishers*
10 East 53rd Street, New York, N.Y. 10022

Copyright © 1993 by Daniel Weiss Associates, Inc.,
and Katherine Applegate
Cover art copyright © 1993 Daniel Weiss Associates, Inc.

All rights reserved. No part of this book may be used or
reproduced in any manner whatsoever without written
permission of the publisher, except in the case of brief
quotations embodied in critical articles and reviews. For
information address Daniel Weiss Associates, Inc.,
33 West 17th Street, New York, New York 10011.

Produced by Daniel Weiss Associates, Inc.,
33 West 17th Street, New York, New York 10011.

First printing: November, 1993

Printed in the United States of America

HarperPaperbacks and colophon are trademarks of
HarperCollins*Publishers*

10 9 8 7 6 5 4 3 2 1

ONE

"Oh, that's awful. It's an abomination. It's not possible that something so horrible could exist." Connor Riordan staggered back through the doorway, holding his hand over his face. "It's a crime against humanity, I tell you. And first thing in the morning!"

Chelsea Lennox glared at him impatiently. "Connor, it's only a dirty diaper. Get a grip." She handed him the used Pampers. "Then get rid of this."

"I can't, Chelsea," Connor pleaded. "I'll feed the little monster, I'll burp it. I'll even bathe it. But I can't—"

"Connor!" Chelsea snapped. "Take the diaper. Take it right now."

"Gak," the baby commented from her position on the coffee table.

Connor wrinkled his face miserably and lifted the corners of the diaper with two fingers. Then, holding his breath, he bolted from the room.

Once Connor was out of earshot, Chelsea allowed herself a groan. "If this is what it's like having kids, I think I'll pass. Permanently. Thank goodness the baby-sitter will be here in a few minutes. I actually look forward to going to work now."

Marta Salgado leaned forward in her wheelchair to pull a fresh diaper from the package. "Here," she said. "Don't forget the powder."

"I mean, it's night and day, night and day," Chelsea continued. "I haven't slept. I haven't gone out. Connor and I are spending half of what we earn on baby-sitters. And it's only been four days. Four days that seem like a lifetime."

"I don't see why Connie should be your problem," Marta said. "I mean, she's Connor's baby. Not yours."

"We don't even know that she's his," Chelsea said firmly. "That's what Molly said, but how much can you trust the word of a woman who'd run off and leave her own baby?"

Marta reached over to tickle the baby's foot. "Are you guys going to do a blood test?" she asked. "We can do it down at the clinic and find out pretty quickly if Connor's the father." She smiled. "Or not."

"Then what?" Chelsea finished diapering and lifted the baby into her arms. "I mean, if she isn't Connor's biological daughter, what do we do? Turn her over to an orphanage? She'll grow up being

2

afraid to ask for more gruel. And when she finally gets out, she'll have to work as a pickpocket."

Marta laughed. "I think orphanages may have improved a bit since the days of Oliver Twist."

Chelsea looked down at the baby with a mixture of affection and annoyance. "You know, when Kate and I came to Ocean City for the summer, I was thinking fun, sun . . . guys with big shoulders. The last great fling before I sentence myself to four years of college, followed by a lifetime of work. I was *not* thinking, Hey, how about if I get engaged to an Irish illegal alien, come within about eight seconds of getting married, and then acquire a baby who may or may not be his?"

"Ahhh bvabva bva bva phh," the baby remarked.

"See, Connie's not thrilled about this, either," Chelsea said. "She's wondering why one minute her mother has pale skin and freckles, and the next minute she's black. This can be very confusing."

"Maybe you should call the cops and have them track Molly down," Marta suggested. She held out her arms. "Here, I'll take her for a minute. You should try to grab some breakfast. But if she dumps again, she's all yours."

Connor came back into the living room, carrying a mug of tea. "We can't call the cops," he said. "For a start, I'm in the country illegally. And then there's the question of where they'd put the baby."

"Chelsea seems to think they'll put her in Dickensian England," Marta joked.

Connor flopped into the aging La-Z-Boy and tilted it back to half recline. He bent over to tie the laces of his work boots. "There's also the question of what they might do to Molly. I mean, she's a crazy, vengeful, stupid girl, but she's not actually evil. I don't believe she means to abandon it altogether."

"It?" Marta echoed.

"He's acting tough," Chelsea said in a loud stage whisper. "When they're alone, he talks goo-goo like everyone else."

"I do not!" Connor cried.

Alec Daniels wandered in from the kitchen. He was wearing a ratty Ocean City Beach Patrol T-shirt and red lifeguard trunks. "I believe the phrase I overheard last night was something along the lines of 'Is Connie-wonnie gonna winky her bottle-wottle?'" He leaned over and gave Marta a kiss on her neck. "Of course," he added, grinning at Connor, "in all honesty, I also overheard the phrase 'Don't you crap again, you little monster. Not if you want to see your first birthday.'"

"Speaking of which," Marta said, wrinkling her nose. She held the baby out toward Chelsea.

"I think it's Connor's turn," Chelsea said.

"Twice in ten minutes?" Connor demanded of Connie. "Twice in ten minutes? You're a bloody spawn of the devil."

"And who would know that better than you?" Chelsea said sweetly.

"Well, Marta and I are going running on the boardwalk," Alec said quickly.

"Running, in his case," Marta amended. "Rolling, in mine. Sorry, Connor. You're on your own."

"I'm in hell," Connor said glumly.

"Gak," Connie agreed.

Justin woke when Kate climbed out of bed to get ready for work. He hadn't heard the alarm, but the movement of sheets and the faint creak of springs had brought him to alertness. He lay still and quiet, enjoying the sight of Kate's body, lit by stray dusty beams of sunlight filtering through the one tiny window in the boathouse. She slipped on her terry-cloth robe and used both hands to tousle her sun-streaked blond hair. Every morning she went through the same routine before she went up to the main house to shower and dress.

"Hi," he said.

"Go back to sleep," Kate said. "You have the day off."

"Unfortunately, that doesn't mean I can sleep in," Justin said, yawning. He hooked his thumb toward his sailboat, rocking gently in the water below the loft. "Job number two." He grinned at her speculatively. "Of course, if you'd like to call in sick and stay here . . ."

Kate shook her head. "I don't think so. Shelby would kill me. We still have all kinds of prep work for the tournament."

"We both work too much," Justin said. "We should play more."

"Well, at least tomorrow you get to work with me on the catch-and-release tournament," Kate said. "That's pretty close to play."

The shark tournament was a big event for the Safe Seas Foundation, where Kate interned. It was an opportunity for the biologists to get a count on the dwindling shark population in the area. Workers from the Foundation and volunteers from the Beach Patrol rode along with fishermen, tagging and weighing all sharks caught and then releasing them back into the Atlantic.

"I'll show you catch and release," Justin said, pulling her close. Kate put up a half hearted struggle, then relaxed into his arms as he kissed her.

He tried to make it last, but she pulled away with a regretful smile. "I gotta go," she said. "Really."

"Don't let Shelby talk you into working late," Justin warned.

"Promise."

He watched her descend the stairway. "Hey," he called, pointing to some papers on the battered table that served as nightstand, dining-room table, and makeshift chair. "You need this stuff you were reading last night?"

Kate stopped on the stairs and glanced over her shoulder. "That? No. That's just some propaganda from Columbia."

Justin rolled out of bed and stretched. Below him, the boathouse door closed behind Kate. He reached for the papers on the table and scanned the top sheet. *Columbia University Freshman Orientation Information*, read the heading. Justin grimaced and tossed the papers aside. It was too early to ruin his day thinking about all that.

He walked across the narrow loft to the railing that overlooked his boat. The sailboat, its mast lying flat, nestled snugly between the wood catwalks, wallowing slightly from the wake of a passing speedboat.

Justin considered going back to bed and enjoying another hour's sleep, but the boat beckoned. A full day to get some work done. He didn't want to waste any of it.

He steeled himself for a cold, cramped shower on the boat. He'd given up using the shower at the house, now that it was even more of a zoo in the morning. Up until recently, Grace, who had shared the downstairs bathroom with him, had never been awake before ten A.M. But now that she worked a day job, he had to compete for access. And competing for bathroom time with a woman, he'd decided, was always a losing proposition.

A shower in his boat involved hunching over

a steel sink in a room the size of a broom closet, head lowered, knees bent, elbows tight against his sides as he worked to aim the hand-held spray nozzle on all parts of his body. The pressure was weak, and the water was cool. Worst of all, he had stupidly mirrored one wall, which meant he had to watch himself while he shuffled and twisted and squirmed.

"Are you *sure* you want to sail around the world?" he muttered as he pried himself out of the shower and slipped on a pair of trunks.

Breakfast was a stale cinnamon bun that he popped in the microwave to soften. He swallowed the last of the roll, then picked up a complicated bit of machinery about the size of his two fists and ventured out into the bright day. Kate's convertible was already gone. He spotted Connor up ahead, carrying his hard hat and all but running from the house. Connor, Justin had observed, had developed a deep love of labor—right about the time he'd been stuck with the baby.

Justin headed south down the main drag. The sun was warm on his back and the breeze was cool. Perfect day-off weather.

Still, there was something about the August sunlight that made him recall that wistful, end-of-summer feeling he used to get as a kid.

Todd's Discount Marine was five blocks away. It was a ramshackle two-story building on the bay, a bait shop in an earlier life. Todd, a beefy, middle-aged man with skin like leather and shockingly white hair, gave him a wave.

"You done with that carburetor already?" he asked.

Justin set the carburetor on the varnished wood counter. "Good as new. My personal guarantee."

Todd nodded. "Well, let's see, that's forty bucks' labor, which I believe knocks down the balance on your account to about five hundred and thirty-two bucks."

Justin winced. "Ouch."

Todd rolled his eyes. "What is it you need today?"

"I need an anchor."

"What for? You never take that boat anywhere."

"Thought I might take her out for a little overnight trip," Justin said. "Run up the coast a ways." He enjoyed the look of surprise on his friend's face.

"Damn, you must have been putting in a lot of hours," Todd said. "And you with that pretty girlfriend. You sure you have your priorities straight?"

"It's not so hard if you just give up sleeping," Justin said.

"It's your life," Todd said. He looked suspiciously at Justin. "If everything shakes down all right, what then? I know you. You're going to be like a bull at the gate."

"The plan is to wait till hurricane season's over, then head south to the Caribbean in October."

"Uh-huh. You're just dumb enough to take off early," Todd said, leaning on the counter. "Don't feed me your bull. Once that boat's ready . . ."

Justin shifted uneasily under Todd's gaze. It was true. Justin was dying to go. It was something he'd worked toward for more than a year, spending every dime on it, every spare minute.

Of course, there was Kate. She was planning on heading off to college at the end of August. But he'd already begun to formulate a plan of his own. He'd get the boat ready, convince her to come along for just the rest of the summer, and then . . . Well, seriously, after she'd seen firsthand how great it was going to be, would she really still want to go to college?

"You going to sell me an anchor or give me a hard time?" Justin asked.

"I can do both at once," Todd said with a laugh. Then he grew serious. "I might have a little suggestion for you, though. You know about the Faial Follies?"

"The what?"

"I take that as a no," Todd said. "It's a race—in the broadest sense of the word. It's mostly weekend sailors and guys with more boat than skill. They start off from Nantucket and make the crossing to Faial."

"Where or what is Faial?" Justin asked.

"It's an island in the Azores chain. About two thousand miles, more or less, due east. All these boats assemble there for a few days of drinking beer and swapping lies, then some head on across to Europe, up toward England or southeast to the Canaries. Usually about a hundred boats or so."

Justin felt his hands clench at his sides. "Cross the Atlantic?" he whispered.

"You and I have sailed together for what, since you were twelve or so?" Todd shrugged. "I wouldn't suggest it if I didn't think you were sailor enough to do it. It's like being on a conveyer belt—you ride the Gulf Stream the whole way. Course, you'll need at least one crew."

Justin swallowed. He wiped his palms against his trunks. *Cross the Atlantic!*

"Anyway," Todd said, "it beats doing something stupid like getting impatient and heading south into the middle of a hurricane. With this race, you'd at least have some company out there. Some dumb-ass real-estate tycoon with a million bucks' worth of boat to haul your sorry butt out of the drink."

"It's something to think about," Justin said, staring into blank space. *Europe!* He could spend the winter sailing the Mediterranean. He and Kate. France, Italy, Greece. How could she say no to that? What better education was there?

"Of course, you'd have to have your boat

11

squared away," Todd said. "They sail from Nantucket in twenty-eight days. And you need time to get up there."

"Twenty-eight days?" Justin echoed.

"Yep," Todd said. He grinned. "Of course, you'll be needing an anchor."

TWO

"What do you want next, young lady?" the cheerful tax attorney asked the next day as he reeled his fishing line out into the water. "White tip? Black tip? Tiger? Maybe a great white?"

Kate sent him a smile. "You've already caught three sharks, Mr. Cutler. That's pretty good for half a day's work."

"Yeah, but no real man-eaters. I don't want to win this contest on lemon sharks alone. I want to see a great white. Maybe a hammerhead."

"As long as it has dorsal fins and teeth, the Safe Seas Foundation will be happy," Kate said. *And as long as it doesn't manage to take a bite out of me while I'm tagging it*, she added silently.

So far, the catch-and-release tournament had turned out to mean hours of lying in the scorching sun on the deck of the big cabin cruiser. The boredom was interrupted only occasionally by moments of great excitement and even fear. Having Justin along should have made it fun, but he'd been oddly preoccupied since yesterday. She'd have thought something was bothering him, although he didn't really seem upset. More like giddy.

Kate rolled over sideways on her towel and resettled her sunglasses on her nose. The sun was blinding. It glittered on every wave crest and shot like laser beams off the polished chrome fittings of the boat. She felt her skin heating up, the SPF 15 lotion almost sizzling like fat in a deep fryer.

Kate could make out the shore two miles back. The boat was too far out for her to see the thousands of bodies on the beach or the thousands more parading the length of the boardwalk. Only the tallest condominiums and the Ferris wheel at the farthest southern tip of Ocean City were clearly visible.

Kate climbed slowly to her feet, feeling woozy from the sun and the gentle rocking of the boat. How these anglers could manage to keep awake while pounding down Miller Lites in this heat was a mystery.

She walked from the bow around the cabin and toward the stern, where Justin stood shooting the breeze with another attorney and an accountant. Justin was wearing a pair of ancient cutoffs and his Ray-Bans. He stood with his arms crossed over his chest, his bare feet planted in a wide stance that adjusted smoothly to the roll of the deck.

"She's just a twenty-eight footer," Kate heard him say.

Naturally, Kate thought with a twinge of annoyance. Justin was talking about his sailboat again.

"I've got a rebuilt Volvo Saildrive in her," he continued. "Picked it up at a salvage for a hundred bucks. Of course, I spent twice that rebuilding it."

The accountant listened with a tolerant, superior smile. "I thought you real sailors didn't believe in engines."

Justin nodded. "Well, I guess we have to believe in them, but unlike you stinkpot drivers, we prefer to use the engine only when necessary. Besides, wind is free. Fuel costs."

"You take her out much?" the attorney asked.

"No. I've been busy doing repairs. I'm thinking I'm about ready for sea trials, though. You know—take her out for forty-eight hours or so, see what breaks."

"Then what?"

From her angle Kate could barely make out the smile on Justin's face. "Then," he said, "if she looks good, it's off toward the open sea."

"Off where?"

"Off everywhere," Justin said. "Sail the world. The Bahamas, the Caymans, Galapagos, Hawaii,

Tahiti." He paused. "I might start with a little race."

Kate felt her heart trip. It was nothing new, of course. She knew Justin's plans for the end of summer. But he'd never mentioned he was thinking of sea trials. Not this soon. No wonder he seemed preoccupied.

"Lucky bastard," the accountant said, shaking his head.

"You going alone?" the attorney asked him.

Kate saw Justin hesitate. "Only if I have to," he said in a low voice.

"You ought to take that blond up there. What's her name?"

"Kate," Justin said. "Yeah, that's the general idea."

"Lucky bastard," the accountant said again.

Suddenly there was a shout from the front of the boat. "Hey, I got a strike up here," Mr. Cutler yelled.

All heads turned toward the stern. Justin's shaded gaze fell on Kate. He crossed toward her.

"How long have you been standing there?" Justin asked.

"Long enough. Why didn't you tell me your boat was ready for sea trials?" Kate said in a low, accusatory whisper.

"You've never been very interested in my boat's progress," he said.

"When were you going to tell me?" Kate demanded. "As you waved good-bye on your way to Tahiti?"

Justin gripped her arms in his strong, callused hands. "I don't want to wave good-bye to you at all, Kate. I want you standing beside me. And I want you with me on the beach in Tahiti, or wherever. You know that."

Kate felt herself melting toward him. His touch had never failed to weaken her. But she shook her head. "Justin, you know that isn't going to happen."

"I don't know anything," Justin said stubbornly.

"Hey, somebody get up here," Mr. Cutler yelled. "I think I got a white tip!"

"We'd better go," Justin said. "We can talk about this later, back at the house." He released her and sidled past.

"You don't believe me, do you?" Kate asked. "In your heart, you think I'll end up going along."

Justin stopped and turned back toward her. "In my heart I believe you love me, and I love you."

"That doesn't mean I'll trade my dreams for yours," Kate said.

"They could be *our* dreams, Kate." Justin smiled sadly. "I know there's room in my boat for you. But your dreams . . . They've never included me."

He pushed past her. Kate felt hot tears start and was suddenly glad for her dark sunglasses.

Grace Caywood slid two perforated plastic cards across the counter to a tired-looking couple dressed in shorts, golf shirts, and new-looking running shoes. "Room 418," she said. "Up the elevator to the fourth floor, turn right, and it will be on your left."

She sighed as she watched them walk away from the desk toward the bank of elevators on the far side of the lobby. Working as a desk clerk was easier than waiting tables. Unfortunately, it was also much duller. Nothing but punching up reservations, verifying credit cards, and handing out keys all day long.

Worst of all, the Ocean City Grand Hotel had an employee dress policy that meant her feet were in perpetual agony. With a furtive check for the manager, she kicked off one pump and rubbed her stockinged toes on the carpet.

Grace checked her watch. One fifty-nine. He'd promised he'd meet her for her lunch break, which began in one minute. And at the O.C. Grand, when they said leave at two, be back at two forty-five, they did not mean two forty-six.

She glanced toward the glass doors that opened directly onto the boardwalk. Compared to the cool, dark lobby, the beach looked like molten silver.

A dark shape appeared in the doorway, silhouetted against the sunlight. Grace couldn't make out the face, but she could see the outline of shoulders and arms and legs, the nonchalant stance, the head held at a slightly mocking angle.

David.

He came toward her, dashing as ever in well-worn jeans and black T-shirt tucked in around his flat, hard waist. He leaned on the counter.

"Got any rooms?"

"Maybe one or two," Grace said.

"I'm very picky," he said.

"Really? I'm sure we have something that you'll like."

"Yes, I'm sure you do," he said smoothly. "But I'd want to look it over first before I decide."

"I could show you something," she suggested.

"Could you? That would be nice."

She selected a key from the drawer before her and came around the counter. "Follow me, please."

"Anywhere."

They walked quickly to the elevator. It was brass, with rows of tiny white lights on the ceiling. The doors closed, and instantly Grace felt David's arm slide around her waist. She tilted back her head, closed her eyes, and returned his long, deep kiss.

The kiss lasted ten floors. They parted as the doors opened, both gasping for air.

Grace led David down the dimly lit hall, carpeted in plush burgundy. It took several tries for her to insert the key and open the door.

They stepped inside without a word. The curtains were parted and the pristine room was half bright sunlight, half shadow. The bed was split right down the middle, light and dark.

David took her head in his hands and leaned down, brushing her lips in a tender kiss. After a moment, he pulled back, holding her at arm's length. Grinning, he looked her up and down.

"Very professional looking," he said.

"Blue suit, white blouse." She shrugged. "Drab is our goal here at the Grand."

"High heels," he said. "I like that."

"Try wearing them."

"I would, but they don't make panty hose in my size." He looked down at her legs, then back up at her speculatively. "*Are* they panty hose?"

"Let me guess," she said. "You're one of those garters-and-stockings types."

"Could be," he admitted. "And what type are you?"

Grace ran both her hands through her shoulder-length dark hair and shook her head. "I like them tall, dark, and handsome," she replied.

"Older?"

"Maybe by a few years," she said. "Say, twenty-one, twenty-two."

"Try saying twenty-six," David suggested.

"Okay, twenty-six." She moved closer and brushed his stubbled chin with the back of her fingers, enjoying the rough feel. David didn't like to shave. He said he'd had to shave twice a day when he was in the Air Force. Since then he tried to keep his rendezvous with the razor to twice a week.

"You never answered my question," David said. He held her tight, one hand cupping her chin. His lips were only millimeters from her own. His other hand traveled ever so slowly down her back, sending shivers through her.

"Which question?"

"Panty hose?"

"Why should I ruin the suspense?"

"I guess I'll have to find out the hard way," David whispered. His hand traveled lower, down her back, and then slid around to graze her thigh.

Suddenly Grace felt her heart beginning to race. She swallowed. Her breath felt labored.

No, not again. No more. It's over, ancient history.

David's lips found hers as his hand reached the hem of her skirt. She kissed him passionately, desperately, praying she would be able to stop the panic that was rising in her.

A dark room, lit by flashes of lightning from the hurricane that raged outside. A bar. The smell of spilled beer and fresh scotch.

"No!" She pushed David away with both hands. Instantly she was ashamed, covering her face with her hands. "Oh, damn, damn, damn."

She collapsed onto the bed, half in shadow.

David let out a curse, but a second later he was beside her, stroking her hair. "I'm sorry, I'm sorry," he whispered. "That wasn't directed at you, Grace."

She took his hand in hers and kissed it. Tears fell hot and fast down her cheeks. "I'm so sorry. I thought . . ."

David put his arms around her, drawing her to him. She laid her head against his chest and cried quietly. "I don't know what's the matter with me," she sobbed.

"Yes, you do, Grace, only you won't tell me," David said, a different kind of frustration in his voice.

"I don't want to," Grace said.

"Do you think there's anything you can tell me that would make me love you any less?" David asked gently.

"It makes me hate myself," Grace muttered. "I don't want it to have the same effect on you."

"Look, the booze makes us all do things we regret. You and me and every other poor dumb jerk of an alcoholic." He pulled slightly away to look in her eyes. "You can tell me, Grace. I won't laugh or sneer. I won't even feel sorry for you."

Grace was silent for a long time, thinking, re-membering. After it had happened, as she'd lain sick and disgusting beneath the boardwalk, David had gone searching for her. And he had stood by her since. Maybe she should tell him. Maybe.

"It's something that happened while I was drunk," she said at last. "During the storm."

He remained silent, listening.

In a forced, cheerful voice she went on. "You know Petie's? It's a bar on the boardwalk."

"Yeah, I know it," David said.

"He, um, Petie, that is—" Grace choked on her words. She bit her lip and struggled to regain the use of her voice. "It wasn't, you know, all the way. He was drinking too. More than me, I guess."

She could feel David take a deep breath and let it out slowly. "Did he hurt you?" His voice was low and bitter.

"It wasn't like that," Grace said. "I . . . I needed a drink, David. You know what that's like."

"Yeah. I do."

"And I would have done—" Again Grace's voice failed her.

"It's okay, sweetheart. It's okay. It was the booze."

Grace shook her head. "No, it's not okay. It . . . Every time I try to . . ." She gathered herself, forcing her voice back under control. "Every time we get close, David, it's like this blanket comes down, smothering me. I panic. I try to stop it, but it . . . it terrifies me."

"Shhh, Grace." He patted her head softly. She nestled into the crook of his arm, letting him treat her like a child, letting him wrap his protection around her.

"I love you, David," Grace said in a whisper. "I love you."

Suddenly she realized she'd never said those words to David before. But then, she'd never said them to anyone but her little brother. Not her father. Not her mother. Not Justin when they were together.

She opened her eyes and looked up at him. "You could still kiss me," she said.

David smiled slightly and leaned down to her. "Yes," he said. "I sure could."

THREE

Kate checked her watch and sighed. Three and three-quarter hours, and Justin still wasn't speaking to her. It was proving to be a very long day.

Fine, she thought angrily. *Let him mope.*

This wasn't their first fight, but they were definitely setting a new record for Longest Sustained Silence in a Confined Space.

She glanced at her other companions on the boat. If she wanted company, she had her choice of the three tanked fisherman or the grouchy captain, a weathered old man from Maine. He was obviously not much of a talker. Thus far, the sum total of their conversation had been "Nice weather, isn't it, skipper?" to which he had replied, "Ayuh." Not much of an improvement over Justin.

Fortunately, by four thirty the three anglers had grown tired and cranky and in need of afternoon naps after a day in the sun. The captain headed toward shore, hugging the beach as he steered for the inlet that opened to the bay.

Kate watched the miles of beach reel past, still sprinkled with die-hard sun worshippers. Most people were already back in their hotel rooms and condos, comparing tan lines and contemplating the night ahead. Kate liked the beach this time of day, when the crowds had thinned and the sand still held the sun's warmth. You could walk along the ocean's edge and almost pretend it belonged to you and no one else. After Labor Day, things would get even better—cool days, empty beaches, quiet nights.

Not that she'd be here, Kate reminded herself with a wistful smile. By September she'd be immersed in a whole new world at college, and all these people who meant so much to her right now—Marta and Alec and Connor and Grace and Shelby—would vanish from her life. Pictures for her scrapbook. Is that what Justin would be to her a month from now?

"Do we have to stay mad at each other?"

Kate spun around, surprised to find Justin so near. "I'm not mad," she lied.

"I'm sorry if I didn't tell you how far along I was with my boat. I didn't think you were interested in her."

"Her." Kate shook her head. "Listen to yourself."

"It's traditional," Justin explained, shrugging. "Boats are always referred to as *her* or *she*."

"And with good reason," Kate said. "Because guys like you think of them as women. Sometimes I think you care more about that boat than me. It's really pathetic."

As soon as she'd spoken, Kate realized she'd gone too far. She was pushing him, trying to get him as angry as she was. And she'd succeeded.

"No, what's pathetic is passing up a chance at adventure because you can't wait to become another automaton," Justin replied, "marching on the path from the best college to the best law school before you finally dive into some Washington law firm and begin your life's work, talking on cellular phones from behind the wheel of your new BMW."

"You know, Justin, someday you're going to have to grow up," Kate snapped. "You can't be a lifeguard forever. You're living in a fantasy world. You really think when you're thirty you'll still be happy sailing your little boat from one island to the next?"

Justin shook his head incredulously. "No, Kate, I'd be much happier getting my GED and going to college, then going to law school and turning into you without breasts. You're absolutely right. Why spend my life sailing the ocean and seeing the world when I could spend it stuck behind a desk with a fifty-dollar silk tie choking the life out of me?"

Kate was about to fire off another sharp exchange, but stopped herself. They'd had this discussion—this argument—before. Each time it seemed to get more heated. Probably because each time they saw ever more clearly how little chance there was for a compromise. The truth was, Kate couldn't begin to imagine Justin sitting at a desk, wearing wing-tip shoes and a gray suit.

"I'm going for a swim," Kate said, crossing her arms over her chest. "The paperwork's all down in the galley on my clipboard."

"We'll be at the dock in twenty minutes."

"I need the exercise." She glared at him. "I'm feeling a little tense right now."

He held up his hands. "Fine. You do whatever you want. Like I could stop you."

Kate slung a leg over the chrome railing and took a fix on the beach. It wasn't more than a quarter mile away. Not even much of a workout. She poised and dived, aiming to get as far from the boat as possible. As she sliced into the cold water, she could hear the muffled underwater churning of the boat's motor.

When she surfaced, the boat was already past, but she saw Justin climbing toward the flying bridge. It almost made her smile. However angry Justin might be, he would watch her through binoculars, keeping a protective eye on her as she swam toward shore.

Kate rolled over and began swimming in strong, measured strokes, using the tallest building on the horizon, the Ocean City Grand, as a landmark. By the time she reached the breakers, she was tired, but the tension in her arms and neck was gone. Her legs felt rubbery as she climbed the beach, fighting the pull of the receding surf.

"Don't tell me, let me guess," a familiar voice drawled. "You swam in from New Zealand."

Kate looked around at the few people on the nearby sand and picked out Grace. She was stretched out on a blanket, leaning against a blue nylon gym bag. As usual, her bathing suit bordered on the illegal. Grace's friend Beth sat a few feet away, her pink limbs spilling from a dowdy green one-piece. Kate hadn't quite figured out the friendship between the utterly mismatched girls. She only knew it had something to do with Alcoholics Anonymous.

"I thought you were working," Kate said a little sourly.

"Got off half an hour ago," Grace said. "I don't work twenty-four hours a day."

"Is that your uniform?" Kate said, cocking an eyebrow at Grace's suit.

"No, I've locked the polyester up." She patted her gym bag. "Now that I'm working a day job, I have to grab the sun whenever I can. And why are you here, rising like . . ." She turned to Beth. "What were those sea girls? Nymphs?"

Beth pursed her lips. "Nymphs is too general. Naiads were nymphs that lived in rivers. Oceanids would be your ocean nymphs."

Grace turned back to Kate. "So why are you here, rising like an oceanid from the sea? I thought you were out with Justin, counting sharks."

Kate nodded. "I was. I wanted to swim in."

"And Justin?" Grace asked innocently.

"He stayed on the boat."

"Justin stayed on the boat," Grace said to Beth. "At this point I have to be thinking there was a fight of some sort."

Beth struggled to her feet, grunting with the effort. "I have a policy of staying out of other people's romantic entanglements. Of course," she added in a wry voice, "I stay out of my own, too."

"You leaving?" Grace asked.

"I don't really tan," Beth said. "If I'm out here any longer, I'll be the color of a hot dog."

"I guess I'll head home too." Grace stood, snatched up her blanket, and stuffed it into the gym bag. Kate fell into step beside them as they trudged across the sand toward the boardwalk.

"So," Grace said, "you want to tell me all about it?"

"Why on earth would I want to tell you?" Kate asked.

"It involves Justin. I've known him longer than you."

Kate winced. It wasn't a fact she liked to be reminded of. "It's nothing," she said.

"Uh-huh," Grace said as they climbed from the hot sand onto the relatively cool wood of the boardwalk. "How's his boat coming along?"

"His damned boat is fine!" Kate yelled. She noticed Grace's triumphant smile and shook her head. "He's getting ready to take it out for sea trials," she admitted.

"Really?" Grace said. "That could kind of push things forward, I guess."

Kate threw up her hands. "I'm beginning to think he's actually serious about this plan of his."

Grace peered at her over the top of her sunglasses. "Of course he's serious. You practically live down in the boathouse with him. I'm guessing you noticed the fact there's a very large boat there."

"It's like arguing with a child," Kate muttered.

"Don't waste your time fighting it," Grace advised. "You'd have to sink that boat to stop him."

"There's a thought," Kate said glumly.

Suddenly Grace laughed. "You know, it's kind of funny."

"Is it?"

"Sure. You used to think *I* was your competition," Grace said. "Now you've seen the real other woman."

Chelsea sat on the end of her bed, legs curled under her, and peered at the baby. Connie was lying in the cardboard box of a case of Guinness, which was serving as a makeshift crib.

The sun was setting in spectacular glory, turning the walls brick-red. Chelsea wasn't interested in the colors, though. This was about light and dark and shades of gray.

She traded her stick of charcoal for one with a finer tip and made several quick, confident strokes on her sketch pad. Fortunately, Connie was on her best behavior, gurgling contentedly as if she were enjoying the sunset.

Chelsea had done several portraits of Connie. After all, she figured, she wouldn't be likely to have an infant model again anytime soon. Before long, she'd be taking art courses at Columbia, drawing her fellow students or professional models, or camping out in any of the numerous art museums, copying the great masters.

But no babies at sunset.

Chelsea finished the sketch and tore it from the pad. She got up, stretching on tiptoes to get the kinks out of her legs, and crossed to Connie, holding the picture up for her to see. "See? It's you," Chelsea said. "I know it doesn't really *look* like you—it's your essence."

Connie remained utterly uninterested, preferring instead to stare at her own toes. "Not much for art, huh?" Chelsea asked. "More into body parts? Well, maybe you are Connor's, after all."

Chelsea opened the desk drawer and slid the pad in. Her eye was drawn to an envelope, addressed in her own handwriting. Smiling ruefully, she picked it up. It was addressed to her parents, stamped but never sealed.

She sat down at the desk and opened the envelope. Chelsea had written it five days ago, the night before what was to have been her wedding day:

Dear Mom and Dad,
How's the weather there? How are the rosebushes doing? Seen any good movies?

And now, with the chitchat out of the way . . . I have to tell you something that is probably going to shock you. No, I'm not pregnant and I haven't joined a cult. However, I *am* married. Or will be tomorrow morning, assuming nothing goes wrong in the next twelve hours.

Chelsea sent Connie a dubious look. "Say, something like my fiance's old girlfriend arrives from Ireland at the last minute with a baby she says is his. To name one extremely far-out possibility."

She refolded the letter and slipped it back in the envelope. "Well, who knows? Maybe I'll still need it someday. At least it will be a very interesting memento," she said, tossing the envelope on her desk.

There was a brief familiar knock on her door.

"Yes," she called out.

Connor opened the door and leaned against

the frame. "Hey, I have to go down to the market, pick up some groceries," he said in his singsong Irish lilt that turned statements into questions. "Can I get you anything?"

"Why don't *I* go to the market?" Chelsea suggested. "I probably need more stuff than you do anyway."

"Who'd take care of the baby?"

Chelsea rolled her eyes. "How about you?"

"What, without you around too? I don't know anything about caring for an infant."

Chelsea felt her jaw beginning to clench. "Connor, it kind of seems to me that for the last few days *I've* been the person doing all the child care around here."

"I'm paying for most of the baby-sitters when we're at work," Connor pointed out. "And I have changed a diaper now and again."

"Actually, all you've done is what I've forced you to do," Chelsea argued. "You've occasionally offered some minor assistance when you couldn't find a way to sneak out of the room."

"I know. How about if we take the baby with us? The fresh air would do it good."

Chelsea fixed him with an angry glare. "Connor, in case it hadn't occurred to you, I am not the person responsible for taking care of Connie. And *stop* referring to Connie as 'it' or 'the baby.' She has a name."

Connor came over and sat on the bed beside

her. He put an arm around her shoulder. "Look, you're right. You've been a saint through all this. But I've got no one else to turn to, have I? I mean, I can't very well ask Kate or Grace to care for the . . . for Connie."

"Wait a minute," Chelsea said, pushing his arm away. "I think something is slowly beginning to penetrate my mind here. You think taking care of babies is only for women, don't you?"

Connor looked startled. "Did I ever say that?"

"No," Chelsea admitted. Then, in a harder voice, she added, "No, you're much too clever for that. You know if you said something like that in front of me, let alone in front of Kate or Grace, you'd be in deep trouble."

"It's not that only women should care for babies, it's that, well . . . men aren't really suited for the job." Connor gulped hard. "That didn't quite come out the way I meant it."

Chelsea got up from the bed and marched over to the desk. She lifted Connie out of the carton and held her toward Connor. Connor kept his hands firmly at his sides.

"Take her," Chelsea ordered.

Connor shook his head. "She'll puke on me."

"Probably," Chelsea agreed. "That's one of the things babies do. They like to vomit."

"This is so unfair," Connor cried in outrage. "That silly twit Molly. This is all her fault. What does she mean, dropping her foul-smelling progeny at my doorstep? If this was supposed to make me bond with this creature of hers, then Molly has seriously miscalculated." He jumped to his feet, boiling with anger, and headed for the door.

"Connor!" Chelsea snapped.

He pretended not to hear her.

"Connor, freeze!"

Connie immediately began to wail.

Connor took a step forward, hesitated, then let his shoulders slump in defeat.

"Nice try," Chelsea allowed. "You almost made it out of the room."

Connor turned back, grinning. "I thought I was quite convincing," he said without a trace of anger. He shook his head. "Unfortunately, my little show set off the baby alarm."

"That's not why she's crying," Chelsea said, enjoying the moment. She handed the screaming infant to Connor, who took her with the utmost reluctance. "She's crying because she has a dirty diaper."

Connor's face paled. "Chelsea, no. You say you love me."

"I'm going to the store," Chelsea said. "When I get back, Connie had better be clean and smelling like nothing but baby powder."

"Is Kate home?" Connor asked hopefully.

"Connor, you and I almost got married," Chelsea said. "If we had, we'd have had kids eventually. What did you think you were going to do then? Or did you even think about it?"

"I thought about the part where we *make* the kids," Connor said, still holding Connie at arm's length.

Chelsea sighed deeply. "I'm telling Kate and Grace *not* to help you in any way," she said. "If Molly doesn't come back, you may end up being a father, Connor. A *single* father. And you might as well start learning right now."

FOUR

"What was that?" Marta asked. She was sitting on the couch beside Alec, leaning against his shoulder while they watched *A Current Affair*. Before Alec could answer, Chelsea came stomping down the stairs, scowling.

"Hi, Chels," Marta said. "Everything all right?"

"Don't help Connor," Chelsea snapped. "He's got to do some of the baby-sitting around here."

Marta smothered a grin. "Okay."

"I definitely won't volunteer," Alec assured Chelsea.

Nodding in satisfaction, Chelsea headed for the door. "And if you see Grace or Kate, tell them the same thing," she called over her shoulder.

Alec grinned at Marta. "See? Don't you wish you lived here? We're one big happy family."

Connie's wailing suddenly got louder. Connor was descending the stairs, awkwardly holding

Connie and making a face of sheer disgust. He spotted Marta and his eyes lit up. "Marta! You look like the sort of person who'd have the full range of motherly instincts."

Marta shook her head. "Chelsea said no."

"Sorry," Alec said quickly, jumping to his feet, "we were on our way out."

"Don't you want to spend some time with little Connie?" Connor pleaded.

"I can *smell* little Connie clear across the room," Alec said. He helped Marta get into her wheelchair. "Besides, we have plans."

They made a quick getaway into the cool evening air. The breeze was heavy with the honeysuckle that grew in profusion along the side of the house. Alec and Justin had promised the landlord they'd trim it last week, but then, Marta knew, they'd been promising him they'd mow the lawn since June.

Alec lifted Marta into the passenger seat of his Jeep, collapsed her wheelchair, and stowed it in the back. It was getting to be second nature to him, she realized. He looked as though he'd been doing it for years.

In fact, it had only been a month since the first time he had picked her up in his powerful, muscular arms. He'd been tentative with her, embarrassed and uncertain. She liked to think he'd trembled a bit at being so near her. She liked to think the strange intimacy of the moment had excited him more than it unsettled him.

She knew it had excited her.

"Where should we go?" Alec asked, climbing behind the wheel and starting the engine.

"What would you like to do?" Marta asked with a trace of suggestiveness in her voice. But the hint went nowhere. Alec just shrugged.

"How about we go for a drive? It's going to be a nice night."

Marta gazed toward the dying sun coloring the sky with a final explosion of orange that faded to blue and star-speckled black. "Okay," she said. "Let's drive."

Alec headed down the street to the main boulevard that ran the whole length of Ocean City. The traffic wasn't as bad as usual, and Alec wove expertly around slow-moving cars with license plates from Pennsylvania and Ontario.

"You know, I wasn't entirely kidding back at the house," Alec said, raising his voice to be heard above the sound of the Jeep's engine and the breeze whipping around them.

Marta captured part of the tornado that was her hair and slipped a band around it. "What are you talking about?"

"You know, about how you should move in."

"Move in," Marta repeated flatly.

"Into the house," he explained. "I mean, no one ever uses the dining room, and it can be totally closed off for privacy. I could build a wheelchair ramp up the front steps to the porch."

Marta stared at him. "Why on earth would I move into your house?"

"It's not just *my* house," Alec said defensively. "It's Kate and Chelsea and Grace and Connor's house. And partly Justin's house—at least kitchen and bathroom privileges."

"I repeat, why would I move into your house? I have a home of my own."

"Not really your own," Alec pointed out. "You live with Luis—I mean, your dad. But you're eighteen. Why shouldn't you have a place of your own?"

Marta was startled at the suggestion. What had put this idea into Alec's head? Then she relaxed into a smile. Oh. Of course. So much for her concern that Alec was starting to take her for granted. "You think it would be more . . . *convenient* for you to have me right there all the time?"

They stopped at a red light. Alec brushed his sun-streaked blond bangs off his forehead. He looked at Marta, puzzled. "What?" he asked.

Marta rolled her eyes. "You think you'd have an easier time getting me into bed."

"No, that's not it at all." Alec actually seemed shocked at the suggestion. Sincerely shocked. As if that were absolutely the last thing on his mind.

"It's not?" Marta asked.

"Of course not. I thought you'd like to get away from your dad for a while. I mean, I can take care of you as well as he can."

Take care of me? Marta turned the phrase over in her mind. She didn't like the sound of it. She gritted her teeth and stared at a pair of sea gulls fighting over a discarded carton of fries on the sidewalk.

"So?" Alec prompted.

"Alec, why would I want to move for one month? I'm going off to college in about thirty days. So are you."

"I know, I know," Alec said, easing the Jeep forward as the light changed. "I thought maybe it would be a way for you to adjust slowly to living more on your own. You know, a transition between living at home and being in a dorm."

"I see. I need a transition."

"Although it's not like you'll be totally alone at college, either," Alec continued. He seemed oblivious to the fact that Marta was getting increasingly annoyed. "After all, I'm going to the University of Cincinnati and you're going to be at the University of Kentucky. It's only an hour and a half drive. We'll be able to see each other, no problem. I figure we can work out our class schedules so I can arrange to take you wherever you need to go."

Marta stared at him, but no, there was no awareness in his face. He had no idea of how incredibly condescending he sounded. Instead he drove along, glancing cheerfully left and right at the restaurants, half-empty bars, and neon no-vacancy signs of the motels.

"I'm curious, Alec," Marta said in a poisonously sweet voice. "How did you figure I'd have managed college if I hadn't happened to meet you this summer?"

He furrowed his brow. "What do you mean?"

"I have a specially equipped van, as you know," Marta said, "and although it's not as much fun as your Jeep, it does the job. I did manage to get around in the world before you happened along."

"Of course you did," Alec agreed indulgently. "But I like taking care of you."

Marta felt her temples begin to throb. There it was again—*take care.* She drummed her fingers on the dashboard. It was all becoming clear now. All falling into place.

Alec had barely made a pass at her in weeks. When they'd first gone out, they'd been all over each other. That first night, when they'd gone for a midnight swim in the secluded lagoon, he'd looked at her with eyes that could have melted steel. Now, he wanted to *take care* of her.

"Take me home," she snapped.

"Home? What for?"

"Because I want to go home," she said. *You jerk*, she added silently.

"Wait a minute." Alec pointed an accusing finger at her. "You're mad about something, aren't you?"

Marta answered him with stony silence. Alec

drove two more blocks and turned right toward the apartment she shared with her father. He parked in front and shifted sideways to look at her.

Damn. She wished she could simply storm away and slam her front door in his face. Instead she reached into the back and clumsily extricated her chair.

Alec jumped out and came around to her side. He took the chair from her and set it up with practiced ease.

She glared at him, then down at the chair. The Jeep was simply too high off the ground. It was not a move she could manage alone.

"Would you give me a hand?" she asked as coldly as she could manage.

Alec lifted her in his arms and set her down in the chair. "Are you going to tell me what I did wrong, or do I have to spend the next day or so guessing?" he demanded.

Marta turned her chair away. *Damn.* He could be so difficult. She spun her chair back to face him, reached up, and grabbed his shoulders. She exerted more pressure than was strictly necessary, but she wanted not to feel helpless. She wanted him to feel some of the strength that came from moving herself around with only her arms. His eyes widened in surprise.

"Hey," he complained.

She drew him down to her. "Listen to me,

44

Alec Daniels. You don't *take care* of me. Do you understand?"

"All I did was ask you to move in with me," Alec protested.

"You asked me to move in so you could *take care of me*. If you'd asked me to move in because you couldn't stand being away from me, because you want me near, because you think in your sleazy mind that if I were right there you'd be able to put the moves on me, *that* I wouldn't mind."

"You wouldn't?"

"I'm not saying it would work." She looked directly into his eyes. "But at least I'd be sure you weren't thinking of me as your burden, your good deed so you can win your Boy Scout be-kind-to-crips merit badge."

"That's not—"

"Look. I'm your girlfriend. I'm not your little sister. Know how you can tell the difference?" Marta pulled his face to her and kissed him hard and slow until he was gasping for air. Then she pushed him away.

"That's the difference, Alec," she said. "Don't forget it again."

"Let's see," Chelsea said as she sauntered along the shore the next afternoon, "I started at ten, minus half an hour for lunch and two breaks, which subtracts another half hour." Chelsea was

45

no longer self-conscious about talking to herself as she walked the beach. Usually she remembered to whisper. Sometimes—like today—she didn't.

"So," she said, "that's six hours of actual time on the beach. Six hours. Fine. It's two hundred yards between lifeguard stands, and I go from Alec's stand down to Melanie's stand, which is a total of eight hundred yards, or twenty-four hundred feet. That means each complete circuit is a little less than one mile."

Chelsea paused to look hopefully at a young couple who'd been asleep on her previous pass. She pointed to the camera bag that hung by her side. "Photograph? Ten-minute video? Preserve this magic moment forever?"

The guy shook his head. Chelsea shrugged and trudged on down the burning sand. This morning, expecting another cool day, she'd made the mistake of wearing one of her hand-painted T-shirts over a pair of biker shorts. Unfortunately, the day had turned into a scorcher.

"Anyway," she continued, "this will make twelve complete cycles, which means I've walked almost ten miles today. Now, if I work five days a week and keep this job all summer—"

"Talking to yourself again, Chelsea?" Alec called out as she neared his chair. He kept his gaze on the water, though only one guy was playing with a boogie board in the moderate surf. Two very tan, very nearly naked girls lay on a

Ren and Stimpy beach blanket a few feet away.

"I'm figuring out that if I keep this job the whole summer, I would walk . . ." Chelsea calculated quickly in her head. "I'd walk over 600 miles. I think."

"Well, as long as you're using your time wisely," Alec said as Chelsea circled the stand and headed back up the beach.

One of the girls, evidently emboldened by hearing Alec speak, got up, tugging at the bottom of her suit. Chelsea watched over her shoulder as the girl went over and leaned seductively against Alec's chair. It was an occupational hazard for lifeguards, although the lifeguards as a rule didn't seem to mind.

Chelsea slid the video camera from her shoulder, aimed, and focused. Through the viewfinder she could see the girl walk back toward her blanket. She zoomed in on Alec, capturing his expression as he watched the girl.

"I'm getting this for Marta," Chelsea yelled.

"Very funny," Alec said. "Hey, come here." He waved her back. "You're a woman."

"Uh-huh," Chelsea agreed guardedly as she returned.

"Well, let me ask you something. Hypothetically."

"Uh-oh. A hypothetical question, huh?" Chelsea squinted up at him. Why did she have the feeling this would be about Marta?

"Is it or is it not the guy's obligation to look out for the girl?" Alec asked as he scanned the water.

Chelsea sighed. What was she? Dear Abby? "Well, what do you mean by 'look out for'?" she asked cautiously.

"I mean look out for," Alec said. "Like the guy protects the girl."

"From whom, or what?"

Alec pondered this for a moment. "Mostly from other guys, I guess. I mean, assuming we're not in the jungle and worrying about leopards."

"Leopards?"

"That would be in the wild," Alec clarified. "In civilization, we protect women from, you know . . ."

"Other guys," Chelsea supplied. "Some civilization."

Alec ignored her. "And let's say," he continued, "the woman is . . . I don't know, blind. The guy would help her cross the street, right?"

Chelsea rolled her eyes. "Why don't we say the woman is in a wheelchair, and her name is Marta. You know, hypothetically."

"My point is, what's wrong with trying to help someone out?" Alec said. "That doesn't mean you're looking down at them, right? It means you care about them."

"So Marta nailed you, huh?"

Alec took in a very deep breath, continuing to

scan his two hundred yards of shoreline, ten seconds left, ten seconds right. "Something about treating her like my little sister," he finally admitted.

That hurts, Chelsea thought. Count on Marta to be blunt. "So don't treat her like your little sister," she suggested.

Alec shrugged helplessly. "How do I do that? Real fast, so she'll forgive me?"

"I don't know. Buy her flowers and take her on a romantic date?"

"Really?" He seemed surprised. "But I see her all the time."

"Maybe that's the problem. You guys shop together and watch TV together. You drive her places. When's the last time you two had a real date?"

"Well, we've only had one, really."

"There you go," Chelsea said. "Less time at the mall, more time gazing into each other's eyes over a candlelit dinner."

"Huh." Alec thought for a moment. "Is that what you and Connor do?"

Chelsea grimaced. "No, what we do is fight over who's going to take care of the baby. Speaking of which, I have to get going. The babysitter takes off at five." She gave a little wave and moved away. "Don't ever have kids," she called back over her shoulder. "You think you have no romantic life now!"

She walked quickly to the boardwalk and

wound her way through the crowds toward the construction site where Connor was working. In front of a swimsuit shop, she paused to check out a rack of sale items. Already the end-of-summer sales were in full swing. Chelsea found a two-piece like Grace's and fingered the price tag. She sighed. She had enough cash, but did she have enough nerve?

"Thirty percent off," said a saleswoman in the doorway.

"I don't think I have the guts," Chelsea said, returning the suit to the rack. "And I know I don't have the thighs."

Chelsea headed on down the boardwalk, comforted by the knowledge that she could always come back later. With all the exercise she'd been getting, trudging up and down the sand every day, she'd been feeling a lot better about her body lately. Not *that* good, but who knew? There were still a few weeks of summer left. In any case, she reminded herself in a sudden fit of annoyance, she needed to hang on to every penny she had right now for Connie's expenses.

As she neared the construction site, she could hear Connor with several of his friends, talking together in varying Irish accents. He spotted her approaching and his face dropped. He tried to cover it quickly with a welcoming smile, but it was too late. She'd seen the look.

"Chels!" he called enthusiastically.

She came over and accepted his quick kiss on her lips. "How was work?" she asked.

"Work is work," Connor said, to the general agreement of his friends.

"Ready to head on home?" she asked brightly.

He darted a glance at his friends. "Um, actually, the lads and I were thinking of heading on over to Sean's for a quick pint of Guinness."

Chelsea smiled coldly. "Oh, but you must have forgotten, *dear*. You have to go home."

Connor flushed, clearly embarrassed, as his friends grinned in enjoyment at his discomfort. "I'll be along shortly," he said tersely.

Chelsea planted her feet and stuck her hands on her hips. "You have certain little matters to deal with at home, Connor."

"Can't you take care of it for a while, and then I'll take over later?"

Right. "No, Connor, I can't," she snapped. "And she's a person, not an *it.*"

Connor's friends were watching the back-and-forth like spectators at a tennis match.

"Sweetheart—" Connor began.

"Don't sweetheart me," Chelsea said angrily. "I am tired of getting stuck doing all the work with Connie. That baby is your responsibility."

"I thought you agreed to help out," Connor said.

"It's women's work, isn't it?" the one named Sean said as if he were stating the obvious.

"It's not *this* woman's work," Chelsea said. "She's not my baby, and unlike you, Connor, I can say that with some certainty, because it's not likely that *my* baby would be born with blue eyes and snow-white skin."

"Half an hour," Connor pleaded.

Chelsea stuck her finger in his chest. "The baby-sitter leaves right at five. I'm *not* going home, at least not for a while. So *you* make up your mind what you're going to do. *Daddy*."

Chelsea spun on her heel and headed straight back to the swimsuit shop. "Here," she said, handing the two-piece to the saleswoman. "Turns out I have the guts after all."

FIVE

Kate opened the boathouse door that evening, expecting to find Justin working on his boat. To her surprise, he was sitting on his bed, leafing through a book of famous quotations. He looked up guiltily when she started to climb the stairs to the loft.

"What are you doing?" she asked.

He jumped up from the bed and came to meet her at the top step. "Preparing."

"Preparing for what?" She kicked off her deck shoes and flopped on the bed with a sigh. She'd spent the second day of the catch-and-release tournament on a cabin cruiser with a man and his wife. Kate had watched them fight and listened to Samantha, the woman who was her Beach Patrol volunteer, complain all day. By late afternoon, only one small shark had been caught, tagged, and released, and the lifeguard had concluded Kate was a traitor to her sex because she refused to endorse the statement that all men are pigs.

If she and Justin hadn't reached a truce yesterday evening, Kate probably would have agreed with Samantha.

Justin seemed frozen between excitement and indecision. Finally he sat down on the bed beside her. "Look," he said, "I've kind of decided something, Kate."

Kate felt herself tense up. She closed her eyes, trying to relax into the sheets.

"Up until now, my plan was to get the boat ready, wait for the end of October when hurricane season is over, then head south to the Caribbean, right?"

"If you say so," Kate answered. The last thing either of them needed was to start a new round of this same battle.

"I figured I'd spend several months, maybe almost a year, down there. Work a little to cover my expenses. Go from island to island, eventually sail through the Panama Canal. And so on. You've never exactly shared my enthusiasm for doing that." Justin grinned. "You don't see the educational value of lying on the beach with a cool drink."

Kate opened her eyes and managed to return his smile. "I guess you could say that. I never said it wouldn't be fun, though. I might have to grow up someday, and I'm not quite convinced that a slow tour of the Turks and Caicos or Grand Cayman is going to do much for me."

Justin nodded in agreement. "So what you're after is education."

"Look, Justin," Kate said, sighing, "are we going somewhere with this, or are we simply heading for the same old fight? Because I had a really long day at work, and I'm sort of tired."

"You want to start in right away on moving your education forward, right?" Justin persisted.

Kate sat up and leaned against the loft railing. "That's right. It's called college."

"You know, Kate, I believe it was Francis Bacon who said, 'Travel, in the younger sort, is a part of education.'"

"You just happen to have been memorizing Bacon."

"You know how I love Bacon," Justin said. "Much better than sausage and almost as much as I love Saint Augustine, who said, 'The world is a book, and those who do not travel read only a page.'"

"I doubt if he was thinking of the Bahamas at the time," Kate said, smiling in spite of herself.

"No, probably not," Justin said smoothly. "He was probably thinking that 'The grand object of traveling is to see the shores of the Mediterranean.'"

"Also Saint Augustine?"

"Samuel Johnson."

"But you're not going to the Mediterranean," Kate pointed out.

"Oh, but I am," Justin said triumphantly.

Kate's breath caught. Europe? Justin was going to try sailing to Europe?

"I wasn't sure at first, but I've been thinking it over. There's a race, so there will be a hundred boats all within a couple hundred miles of each other." Justin hunched forward, speaking rapidly and persuasively. "It will be like driving on the freeway. Prevailing winds, strong current. It'll be easy. Hell, I'm far more experienced than a lot of the guys who'll be making the crossing."

"But Europe?"

"Yes! As in Spain. As in France. As in art and architecture. As in Greece, the cradle of the West. As in ancient ruins. As in history. I looked at your Columbia catalog, Kate. You're thinking about signing up for an introductory course on European history, right? You want to learn it from a book or from being there? You want to read about the early Greek city-states, or do you want to walk around them, eating feta cheese and drinking retsina?"

"Europe," Kate whispered, turning away from Justin's intense, questioning gaze. She'd thought very seriously of traveling there this summer, but had decided to come to Ocean City instead. It was cheaper, and if the truth were told, she'd harbored some secret hope of running into Justin again.

Europe! It was like hearing someone mention chocolate when you were starving. It was a word loaded with every possible seduction. And Europe with Justin!

She could make it a great educational experience, couldn't she? Read Shakespeare in England, Dante in Italy, Voltaire in France? Why not Aristotle in Athens?

Wouldn't that be better than college?

Kate realized Justin was still staring at her hopefully.

She lifted her hands, palms raised. "I don't know," she said.

"But you'll at least consider it?"

She hesitated. What was worse—to dash his hope now, or to give him false hope only to dash it later?

And *was* it only false hope? An image was coming to her—a sailboat at anchor in Piraeus harbor a few miles from Athens. She was with Justin, the two of them wearing loose white cotton clothing as they prepared to take the dinghy into shore for a day of sightseeing . . .

An alternate vision came right behind that one—a vision of her, alone at a carrel in a stuffy, overheated library, surrounded by mountains of books.

"Kate?"

She realized she hadn't answered Justin, and when she focused on his face, she detected a note of triumph in his smile. "No answer necessary," he said. "You're *already* thinking about it."

She grabbed him roughly by the front of his T-shirt. "You think you know me so well. Maybe I was thinking about something else entirely." She leaned forward and kissed him on the lips, but he pulled away, laughing.

"Hey, no time for that. If we're sailing for Europe in a few weeks, I have a lot of work to do."

Kate emptied the plastic basket into the washing machine and twisted the knob. Her panties and T-shirts barely filled a third of the load, so she glanced around for something else to add. A small pile of faded red Beach Patrol trunks mixed with underwear lay close by. Either Alec's or Justin's. She lifted one of the pairs of underwear. BVD. Justin's. Alec was a Fruit of the Loom man. Connor wore plaid boxers.

She dumped Justin's dirty clothes in on top of her own and measured out the detergent. Odd, that she had actually reached the point where she could tell whose underwear belonged to whom. Bright colors, in any number of styles, meant Chelsea. Grace went with French-cut silk. Her own, of course, were all cotton, in whites and pastels.

It was late, and she worried that the noise of the washing machine might wake Chelsea and the baby, who were asleep upstairs. But she had no choice—she'd run out of clean things to wear. Besides, she needed something to do to keep herself occupied. Ever since Justin had dropped his big Europe news on her earlier that evening, she'd been bouncing around like a coiled spring.

She headed to the living room, snagged the remote from the coffee table, and flopped down on the couch. The clock on the VCR showed eleven fifteen. Soon Letterman would be on. She smiled contentedly. She could watch TV and do her laundry, and to hell with Justin if he wanted to spend half the night working on his boat. Maybe she would spend the night in her *own* room for a change. That way she could stall any more discussion about going with him to Europe.

She heard the loud *thunk* as the old Maytag started its wash cycle. She waited to hear a corresponding screech from upstairs, but apparently the baby was still asleep. At least for now.

Kate thought *she* had problems. What on earth were Chelsea and Connor going to do about the baby? Already the strain of foster parenthood was beginning to show on both of them. At dinner that night, they'd barely exchanged a word.

"AHHHHH AHHHH AHHHH!"

The cry electrified Kate. She sat bolt upright and looked around the darkened room. It wasn't the baby she'd heard. The noise had come from Grace's room, the only downstairs bedroom.

Kate ran down the hall and pressed her ear to Grace's closed door. She heard a whimpering sound and knocked lightly, but there was no answer. Finally, unable to walk away, Kate eased opened the door.

Grace was tossing violently in the bed, making a sound that was heartbreaking to hear. Kate leaned down and touched her bare shoulder. It was covered with goose bumps.

"Grace," Kate said. "Grace, wake up. You're having a nightmare."

Suddenly Grace fell still. Then, after a long, silent pause, Kate heard a string of muttered four-letter words.

"You were having a nightmare," Kate repeated.

"Yeah, I noticed," Grace said in a weary voice. "Was I talking in my sleep?"

"Yelling."

"Oh." Grace sighed and sat up, pulling a spare pillow behind her back. "Damn, I wish I could have a drink."

Kate said nothing. Hopefully, Grace wasn't serious about wanting a drink. Or at least not serious enough to try to take a drink. She supposed alcoholics pretty much always *wanted* a drink.

Grace seemed to have read her mind. "Don't worry, Golden Girl. I'm not going to go raid Connor's beer supply."

"Golden Girl?" Kate repeated.

"Sorry. I'm in a pretty vicious mood," Grace said. "Thanks for waking me up. I hope I didn't scare you. I'll try not to do any more midnight screaming."

"It's only eleven twenty." Kate started to leave, but somehow the notion of Grace, sitting silent and alone in her bed as she sorted through the memories of some private terror, made her turn back. "You know, Grace," Kate said softly. "I have this recurring dream. This recurring nightmare."

"Yeah?" Grace's voice was neither inviting nor rejecting.

Kate came closer to the bed, standing awkwardly in the dark, glimpsing Grace as a mere shadow within shadows. "It comes whenever I'm under stress of some kind. Like when I first came to O.C. Other times too, like after the hurricane."

Grace remained silent. The only sound was a slight shifting on the sheets.

"It's always the same," Kate continued. "I don't yell or anything. But when I wake up, I realize I've been crying in my sleep."

Grace sighed. "You're not trying to bond with me, are you, Kate?"

Kate felt a flush rise in her cheeks. "Fine. Screw you, Grace."

Grace laughed softly. "I am a bitch, aren't I?"

"Yes."

"I've thought about trying to change, but I think it may be my core personality."

"Well, don't worry about my feelings." Kate allowed herself a short laugh. "I'm getting used to you."

For a while they were both silent. Then Grace spoke again. "I'll tell you mine if you tell me yours."

"Aren't you afraid we might bond?" Kate asked mockingly. "I wouldn't want you to feel our mutual distrust was in any way weakened."

"I don't distrust you," Grace said. "I like a little tension in my relationships, though. Wouldn't it be awfully boring if you and I were just bosom pals, giving each other home perms and gossiping about boys? We've shared the same man, after all. I think that calls for something a bit more ambiguous."

Not for the first time Kate marveled at the voice coming out of the blackness. Drunk or sober, feeling great or afraid, Grace remained Grace. "Mine's about my sister," Kate said at last.

"I didn't know you had a sister."

"She died."

Again a silence stretched between them. "Come here," Grace said. "Have a seat."

Kate found the edge of the bed and perched on it. Her eyes were growing accustomed to the dark, and now she could see the faintest outline of Grace's head, the occasional glimmer of her eyes.

"Juliana. She . . ." Kate fought the quaver in her voice. She knew it was coming, but she still couldn't say it without feeling her throat tighten. "She took a handful of pills . . . she committed suicide."

Grace waited patiently.

"I found her," Kate continued. "On her bed. And that's what I dream about."

Grace cursed, softly, bitterly.

"Yeah," Kate agreed. "That's about right." She waited for Grace to make the usual noises of reassurance, the familiar *Life goes on, you have to focus on the good memories, at least you had her for a while* blather. Or else the inevitable question, the one Kate could not answer—*Why?*

"Not such a Golden Girl," Grace said with gentle humor. "You have secrets of your own, and I never even suspected."

Kate picked up her tone. "We blonds are never suspected of having any depth."

"Try taking up serious drinking," Grace said. "People automatically assume you're concealing some great tragedy." She sighed. "In this case, it's not as much a tragedy as a comedy. A variation on the question of whether you should fool around with a guy because he bought you a nice dinner. Except in my case it wasn't dinner, it was scotch."

Kate listened with growing shock as Grace told her what had happened in a dark, deserted bar while Hurricane Barbara had pounded Ocean City.

"You should have him arrested," Kate said.

"For what? Giving booze to a minor?" Grace's voice had lost its usual smooth assurance. "See, he didn't force anything on me, Kate. That's not what this story is about. This is a story about what a drunk will do . . . what *I'll* do . . . for a drink. It's a fine story of self-degradation. Loss of pride."

"He's still a piece of crap on two legs," Kate said.

"No argument there."

"And he still used you when you weren't exactly fit to make sensible decisions."

"Yeah. I'm sort of afraid I'll run into him," Grace admitted in a sad voice. "I avoid that whole end of the boardwalk. I feel he has this power over me. He knows my weakness." She sighed. "Beth says I should forget it. David . . . well, I had to make him promise not to kill Petie."

"I don't think you can let David handle this for you," Kate said. "As much fun as it would be to watch."

Grace sighed. "It all comes down in my mind to that moment when Petie put the drink in front of me and I couldn't say no," she muttered. "I can't stand the fact that I can't say no."

"You could say no now," Kate said confidently.

"Could I? Maybe. Not everyone is as strong as you are, Golden Girl Kate."

"I think you learn to be strong when you have to," Kate said, remembering the year it had taken her to begin to deal with Juliana's death. "And I think this is your time."

Grace fell silent for a long while, and Kate waited, letting her own memories float past.

"Damn," Grace said finally. "I have this terrible feeling we just bonded."

Six

"You know, Connie, I can still remember the days when a day off did *not* mean playing chase the sucker with you," Grace said as she bent down the next morning to pick up the pacifier for the seventh time. She inspected it for dirt before sticking it back in the baby's mouth.

"Used to be I had a day off work, I'd head down to the beach, work on my tan, flirt with lifeguards." Grace stuck her arm in the baby's face. "See? I'm nearly as pale as you. Although I certainly smell a lot better."

Why on earth had she volunteered to take care of the baby? Connor and Chelsea were stuck, but that didn't mean she had to be.

"What are we going to do with you, kid?" Grace asked. "I mean, no one around here is exactly parent material. Not that your real mother is, either. I guess no matter how it works out, you're going to be a kid raised by kids."

Suddenly Grace stopped and snapped her fingers. Wait a minute. Chelsea never said Connie couldn't go to the beach. Why not? Slather on plenty of maximum-strength sunblock, rent a beach umbrella to put over her, why not?

"Beach baby," Grace said delightedly. "We'll take you right down and plant you in front of Uncle Justin. Oh, he'll love that, won't he?"

Quickly Grace changed into a bathing suit. Nothing too provocative, she decided with some regret. If she was going down by Justin's chair, well, she needed to keep in mind that she and Kate had bonded last night. Sort of. Besides, she was going to have a baby with her. Somehow skimpy bikinis and babies didn't seem to go together.

She gathered diapers, bottles, pacifier, spare pacifier, powder, lotion, and box of Baby Wipes. "Okay, now where's that thing of yours? That baby-carrier thing your rotten mother left behind?"

"Agh bvabva," Connie offered.

"You don't know? What good are you?" Grace made sure Connie was secure on the couch, then ran up the stairs to Chelsea's room. The carrier was on Chelsea's desk. She grabbed it and trotted back downstairs. Halfway down she noticed an envelope, stuck to the bottom by a half-eaten Jolly Rancher.

As she was prying it loose, the telephone rang. Grace tossed the letter on the coffee table and grabbed the phone on the fourth ring. "Yes, and make it good," she said.

"Is this where Connor Riordan is staying?"

Grace didn't recognize the voice, but she immediately guessed whose accent it was. "Is this Molly?"

"Is Con there?"

"No," Grace said, "but don't hang up!"

"I'm not hanging up," Molly said, managing to sound indignant. "I want to speak to Connor."

"He's at work."

"When will he be home?" Molly asked. "I need to speak to him, but I've got somewhere I have to go in an hour, so if he's not home by then, I guess I'll ring back tomorrow."

"NO!" Grace shouted. "No," she repeated more calmly. "I'm sure he wants to talk to you." *And roast you slowly over hot coals,* she added silently. "He'll be here in an hour. I can promise that."

"I wouldn't want to put you to any trouble," Molly said.

Too damn late for that, Grace thought. "No problem. He'll be here. One hour. Make sure you call back."

Grace hung up and ran out the door. She was halfway down the block before she remembered the baby. She ran back, strapped Connie into her carrier, stuffed the necessary supplies into a shoulder bag, and dashed out onto the street.

Justin spotted her running down the beach.

At first she looked like someone with a serious limp. She was hobbling. A beautiful girl, wearing a bikini and hobbling at top speed across the sand. Then he noticed that she was carrying something in her arms, while a shoulder bag flopped wildly with every unbalanced step.

Grace? he wondered.

As she drew near, he could see that she was carrying the baby. He sighed. "Now what?"

Grace arrived seconds later, panting and cursing a blue streak. She sat the baby on the sand, draped a towel over her carrier, and flopped back on the sand. "Why the hell do you let people bring bottles onto the beach? I smashed my toe on a Raspberry Snapple, damn it, and it feels like it's broken. Have you seen Chelsea? Get Chelsea! I wasted twenty minutes looking for Connor, but who knows which construction site he's on? I went to three and all I did was get whistled at. What kind of a toad would proposition a woman with a baby?"

"Grace," Justin said calmly. "Is something the matter?"

Grace sat up. "That nutcase of Connor's called. Molly. She wants to talk to him. She's calling back in an hour, only now it's just twenty-four minutes. I can't find him. We need Chelsea!"

"Molly!" Justin stood up on his chair and lifted his semaphore flags. They were for sending messages from one chair to the next, but he'd never had much use for them. He looked down at Grace. "Is Chelsea spelled with EA or EY?"

"Hey, Chelsea!"

She stopped walking and spun around. Someone had called her name.

"You're Chelsea, aren't you?"

It was one of the lifeguards, a girl Chelsea had only spoken to once.

"Yes," Chelsea said.

"Thought so. The message said 'Send Chelsea. Black girl with cam.' I figured that meant the black girl with the camera."

"Send me where?"

"Down the beach," the lifeguard said, pointing to the south.

Chelsea shrugged and started walking. It had to be something important. Justin's area was to the south, which probably meant the message had come from him. Either that or from Alec.

Connor! Connor had been hurt!

That had to be it. He'd fallen off the building or been run over by an earth mover.

She broke into a run, crying as she flew across the sand.

"And he-e-e-e-e-re she comes," Justin said, imitating a race track announcer. "The little filly is coming on strong in the stretch. Whoa! Look out for that sand castle."

"You sure it's her?" Grace asked anxiously, following the direction of his gaze.

"You think there are a lot of black girls with cams running down the beach?"

Chelsea nearly ran past them before Grace could snag her arm.

"Is he okay?" Chelsea blurted.

"Who?" Grace asked.

"Connor, who else? Is he hurt?"

Grace shook her head. "That's not it," she said.

"My parents? The baby? Kate? My bro—"

"Molly," Grace interrupted. "She called."

Connor loaded the last of the sacks of cement powder into the wheelbarrow. He spit on his hands, rubbed them together, seized hold of the handles, and propelled the heavy wheelbarrow forward across the bare concrete of the hotel's fifth floor. He had only gone a few yards when he heard what sounded like a distant angel's voice calling his name.

He set the wheelbarrow down and looked around. There was no one on the floor but a half dozen of his fellow workmen. None of whom had an angelic voice.

He settled his shoulders and lifted again. He'd gone only two feet when the voice cried again, this time in stereo. He stopped and gazed around uncomfortably.

"Too much sun," he muttered. He prepared to

lift the wheelbarrow a third time when he heard the voices more clearly. The tone was still angelic. Only this time, quite clearly, he heard them cry, "We're down here, you moron, are you deaf?"

Connor was the first one through the door, followed closely by Chelsea, still hauling her camera and panting as if she might pass out at any moment. Grace hobbled in behind them, carrying the baby, a towel over her head. The three of them stopped dead in their tracks and stared at the phone.

"Nice entrance," Kate commented. She was standing by the coffee table, stuffing an envelope into her purse. "I'm on my way to run some errands. Thought I'd hit the post office, then stop by the mini-mart to pick up some extra hot dogs for the barbecue tonight. Anyone need any—"

"Two minutes," Grace gasped.

"Has it rung?" Connor demanded.

"No," Kate said.

Connor, Chelsea, and Grace sighed in unison.

"I gather you're expecting a call?" Kate asked.

Connor grinned. "I'm going to strangle her right through the phone. No jury in the world will convict me."

A moment later, the telephone rang. Connor leapt for it.

"Hello," he said tensely.

"Con? That is you, isn't it?"

Connor nodded. "Of course it's me."

"How's Connie, then?" Molly asked.

"She's wondering what the hell became of her mother!" Connor said, unable to keep his voice from rising.

"Don't be silly," Molly said, sounding utterly unperturbed. "She's too young to know one person from the next."

"Where are you, Molly?" Connor asked. If she said Ireland, he was going to kill himself.

"New York, as I said I'd be," Molly said. "I'm staying with my mum's sister and her husband. Fiona and Gerald Dane. I told you I would be, didn't I?"

"Yes, you did," Connor said, struggling to rein in his anger. "Only the Danes have an unlisted phone number. And what with there being more than a few people in New York, we didn't think we'd be likely to find you by standing on a street corner and yelling your name."

"Unlisted? Why would someone do that?"

"This is America, not Ireland," Connor explained. "They do all sorts of odd things. They each have three telephones in their home, one in the car, and another one for walking around with, and then they get annoyed when someone calls." He shrugged an apology at Chelsea. Well, it was true.

"Anyway, Con, I seem to have made a mistake."

"A mistake."

72

"Actually, yes. I've realized that you aren't Connie's father after all."

Connor took a moment to absorb the information. "You suddenly realized that, did you?" he asked skeptically. "How is it you came to *realize* that? I mean, I tried to get you to *realize* that, but no, you were dead certain."

"I don't think we need your sarcasm," Molly chided. "It's just I've realized it was someone else."

"Who?"

Molly hesitated for a moment. "Well, if you must know, it was Tim Moynihan."

"Tim?" Connor sneered in disbelief. Then a light went on in his head. "Tim, was it? Not Tim whose parents happen to have immigrated legally to the U.S.?"

"His parents are here in America," Molly confirmed.

"And Tim?"

"Well, once he was done with school, it was only natural he'd want to join his parents," Molly said defensively.

"So Tim's in the States. Legally?"

"They wouldn't keep a lad separated from his family, now, would they?" Molly said, as though it were obvious. "He's living with them in New Jersey. It's quite near where I'm staying right now."

"Molly, I have to apologize," Connor said. "I always thought you were unbalanced. Now I see you're simply ruthless."

"Tim wants to marry me," Molly said. "And he'll accept Connie as his own."

Well, Connor thought. *There it is—liberation.* "You'll be coming down, then?"

"Not for a couple of weeks," Molly said. "I twisted my ankle rather badly. Stupid of me, I know. I can't travel right now. I was hoping you'd be able to bring her to me."

"Me, go to New York?" The thought was unsettling. It would mean taking time off from work, losing wages, maybe even losing his job. And he didn't have a car *or* a driver's license, so he'd have to fly or take a bus. Worst of all, he'd have to see Molly again, and that could easily lead to murder.

"I don't see how I can, Molly. I can't drop everything here and drag a baby to New York."

"Well, then, I suppose you'll have to keep her a while," Molly said.

Connor felt a hand on his shoulder. He turned and saw Kate. "I'll take her," she whispered.

"What?" Connor asked, putting his hand over the receiver.

"I said I'll take Connie to New York."

"Are you crazy?"

"No," Kate answered. "I have my reasons."

Connor shrugged. "All right, then, if you're sure." He uncovered the receiver. "I seem to have found a way, Molly. Give me your address and phone number."

SEVEN

"What is it—*barbecue* with a *c-u-e*, or *Bar-B-Q* with the hyphens and the capital *q*?" Connor asked. He turned a burger with a long-handled spatula. Falling grease hit the hot charcoal and sent up a brief spurt of flame.

"There are about ten different spellings," Kate said distractedly from her position on the top step of the porch. She glanced anxiously in the direction of the sidewalk, waiting for a sign of Justin. He was half an hour late, which probably meant a stop at a marine-supply shop or a hardware store on the way home.

Chelsea was down on the lawn, playing with the baby on a blanket she'd spread out. Now that the prospect of returning Connie to her mother was more certain, Chelsea seemed to have relaxed a little.

Kate wished she could relax, too. Unfortunately, she did not expect the evening to go well.

Grace pushed the front door open with her foot. She was expertly balancing two plates piled with sliced onions, tomatoes, cheese, and lettuce in her left hand. In her right she held ketchup and mustard.

"Waitress skills," she said. "I knew they'd come in handy someday." Grace set the food down on a card table near the grill where Connor was supervising the turkey franks and hamburgers. She waved to David, who was throwing a Frisbee to Justin's dog, Mooch, in an attempt to distract him from a raid on the ground beef.

"Where's the rest of it?" Connor asked Grace. "Some of these burgers are ready."

"The rest of what?" Grace asked.

"The buns," Connor said. "I have no buns."

Grace headed back toward the house, pausing to pat Connor's behind. "Sure you do, Connor. Not great buns, but they'll do."

"I saw that," Chelsea called out.

"I was thinking of you the whole time," Connor protested.

Kate heard whistling coming from around the corner. A moment later, Justin appeared.

"Hey, what's the deal? Barbecue?" he asked. "We're going to break our nearly unbroken record of pizza? The Pizza Hut delivery guy's going to have a nervous breakdown."

"How do you spell barbecue?" Connor asked.

Kate jumped up to give Justin a quick, welcoming kiss.

"Now there are some buns," Grace remarked. She held up two packages of hot dog and burger buns and gave Kate an angelic smile.

"So how'd the big Molly panic work out?" Justin asked.

Kate pulled free. "I need to talk to you—"

"She's in New York," Chelsea answered.

"What's she going to do?" Justin asked as he bent down to scratch Mooch's head. "Hey, boy. Steal any burgers yet?"

"Justin, I kind of wanted to talk to you about that," Kate said.

"She wants us to bring Connie to her," Chelsea said.

"Thank God," Connor muttered.

"So we're going," Grace said.

"We?" Justin shot a glance at Kate.

Kate hung her head. "We thought we'd drive up this weekend. Take my car. Grace's Miata would barely hold the baby's diapers."

Justin's eyes darkened. "Kate, I was still hoping we could take the boat out for sea trials this weekend."

Kate edged away from the rest of the group, easing toward the water. Justin hesitated, then followed her.

"Look, Justin, before you get mad at me, I have to tell you something," Kate said. "It's a long story, but if we don't take the baby to New York, Chelsea and Connor could be stuck with her for weeks."

"That's their problem, not yours," Justin said. He shook his head angrily. "Damn it, Kate. I thought you were really going to give me a chance."

Kate bit her lip. "Justin, this is a major decision, all right?"

"And going with me for sea trials would have given you a chance to see how you feel about being on a boat with me," Justin argued. "Instead, it's off to New York." He rolled his eyes. "Oh, of course. How stupid of me. New York equals Columbia. That's why you're going."

"That's right," Kate agreed. "I want to visit the campus again, since I happen to have this opportunity."

"So my little idea has already been dismissed?"

"You have it exactly wrong," Kate said softly. "See, I don't need to go this weekend with you, Justin. I don't need to know whether I'd enjoy being on your boat with you. Of course I would. I'd enjoy being on a sinking life raft, as long as you were there."

Justin's eyes softened. "Oh."

"If you'd stop being a jerk for a minute, you'd realize that what's happened is that I'm actually, seriously considering what choice to make. I want to think about it. I want to examine all my options very closely. You, Columbia . . ." She smiled. "Of course, I've already examined you closely."

Justin took her arms and drew her close. "Not today, you haven't."

"Like I'm going to be nice to you after you jump down my throat like that?" Kate asked.

"Kiss and make up?" Justin said, nuzzling her cheek.

"Food's ready," Connor shouted.

Kate pushed Justin away. "How about eat and make up?"

"Mooch!" several voices cried at once. Kate caught a flash of the dog tearing past with a hot dog sticking out of his mouth like a cigar.

"That's my boy," Justin said proudly. He took Kate's arm and they rejoined the others, who were already applying condiments to well-charred meat.

"Where's Alec?" Grace wondered, glancing around.

"Why, more bun patrol?" Chelsea asked.

Kate heard the side door open quietly. Alec was trying to tiptoe around the back of the house unobserved. But Justin had spotted him, too. "Hey. It's wearing a shirt."

"It's wearing a shirt with a collar," Connor added.

Alec tried to raise a middle-finger salute, but the hand he used was holding a rose.

"Aw," David said condescendingly, "isn't that sweet?"

"He's bringing Marta a cute wittle flower," Connor jeered.

Alec paused, a subtly malicious smile on his lips. "I think flowers are a good way for a man to express his love. I mean, I'm sure you've brought your girlfriend flowers before, haven't you, Justin?" His grin broadened. "Connor? David?"

"Actually, it *is* kind of sweet," Kate said. She turned on Justin. "How come you never bring me flowers?"

"Yeah," Grace demanded of David.

"Connor, why can't you be as thoughtful as Alec?" Chelsea joined in.

Alec sniffed his rose, then straightened his collar. "Mess with me, huh, boys? Better think twice next time."

"A limousine?" Marta asked.

"Hey, I have the whole evening planned out," Alec said proudly. "Just like a Love Connection date." He handed Marta the rose and wheeled her from the front door of her apartment toward the white Lincoln stretch limo. "So, where's Luis, anyway? I was terrified he'd be here to observe."

"Daddy? He's with an old buddy of his who has a cabin in the mountains," Marta said. "Fly fishing." She grinned as the limo driver opened the door for them.

"Out of town, eh?"

"I probably shouldn't tell you this, but he won't be back till tomorrow."

"Really?" Alec said, grinning mischievously.

"Luis gone, and you all to myself. Well, well." He helped Marta from her wheelchair onto the broad leather seat of the limousine. "Incidentally, you look stunning this evening."

"Thanks. And you . . . wearing an actual shirt."

"With a collar." Alec tugged at the point of his collar. "I wouldn't want you telling Chuck Woolery I dressed like a slob."

The limousine took them from Marta's apartment to The Claw, the upscale and rather expensive restaurant where they'd gone on their first date. They had crab imperial, rockfish, and strawberries with fresh whipped cream for dessert.

Halfway through dinner, Alec began to realize he really should thank Chelsea for her advice. It *was* different, being on an actual date with Marta. How quickly he had come to take her for granted and define their relationship in terms of need rather than romance.

It had been a while since he'd seen her in a dress like this one—black, low-cut, and form-fitting. Her silver and turquoise jewelry caught the candlelight. Her wavy dark hair hung in loose curls around her face. She didn't need the candlelight to make her beautiful, but it did help to focus his attention on a face that he hadn't paid enough attention to.

After dinner, they rode around town in the limousine, playing the part of millionaires, trying to top each other in making snide remarks about the tourists—the little people—they passed. Later, when the limo swerved to avoid a bicycle, Marta was thrown into Alec's arms, and suddenly the teasing and pretending and idle gossip all vanished in a kiss that went on forever.

The limousine stopped in front of Marta's apartment and the driver came around the side to open the door. He pulled the wheelchair out and began to set it up.

"Wait," Alec said. "Don't bother. Do me a favor and set it on the porch by the front door." He knelt in front of Marta, slid his arms behind her back and beneath her legs, and lifted her easily from the leather seat.

Marta buried her face in his neck. "This is a nice way to travel," she murmured.

At the door she reached down with her key and inserted it in the dead bolt.

"Are you sure your dad is out of town?" Alec asked. "I don't want to suddenly find myself standing face to face with him while I've got you in my arms."

"He wouldn't say anything," Marta said with a laugh.

"No. He'd just give me that death stare of his till I turned to stone."

Inside the apartment, Alec was surprised at how awkward he felt. At Marta's direction, he sat her on the couch. She winced at the harsh light from the overhead bulb and sent him to the kitchen for a candle. He found it quickly and set it on the coffee table.

"Would you, um, like anything else?" Alec asked, still fighting the urge to search the house for signs of Luis.

"Would you?" Marta countered, sending him a smoldering look.

Alec glanced over his shoulder.

"He's in the mountains," Marta said as she lit the candle. Then she grinned. "Why are you so scared of him?"

Alec shrugged and sat down beside her. "I don't know. He's a foot shorter than I am. I have fifty pounds on him. Maybe it's the way he keeps saying 'If you ever hurt my daughter, *I'll kill you*.' Maybe that has something to do with it."

"He's only kidding."

"No he's not," Alec said.

"Okay, he's not," Marta admitted.

Alec took Marta's hand and kissed her fingers gently. The candlelight glimmered in her eyes. "To tell you the truth, both of you intimidate me. I mean, your dad . . . The first time I met him, he had his shirt off, and of course the first thing you see is that scar. And right away you know what made it. And you start thinking this little guy was *in the mouth* of a great white shark. You can look at Luis and count the teeth. And then you start thinking, damn, we're talking a sixteen-foot shark. And this little guy's grinning and acting like it was the funniest thing that ever happened to him." Alec shook his head. "You're both survivors. Him of a shark, you of a bullet."

"I don't have any bite marks on me," Marta said softly, exploring his face with her fingers, then running them through his hair and around the back of his neck.

"Are you sure?" Alec asked. "I haven't checked all of you."

"Yet."

Alec gulped again. He couldn't help himself. Then, embarrassed by his reaction, he began to blush.

Marta laughed, enjoying his discomfort. "Haven't you ever survived anything, Alec?"

Alec tried to think, but Marta's fingers were slowly descending his throat, sliding through the front of his shirt. "I, uh, I . . . I had my appendix out."

Marta shook her head in mock pity. "Poor baby." She unbuttoned his shirt and bent close, kissing his chest. Then down his chest, tender, exploring, until she touched the two-inch scar on his side. He shivered as she kissed him there. "Does that make it all better?" she whispered.

Alec tried to answer, but found that his voice was no longer working.

"I need you to carry me somewhere," Marta said.

"Where?" Alec asked in a strangled, high-pitched voice.

Marta answered without saying a word.

EIGHT

Chelsea sat the baby on the kitchen counter in her carrier.

Connie was in a quiet mood, a contented half-sleep occasionally interrupted by a few gurgles. Chelsea stroked the baby's tiny head, marveling once more at the silkiness of her thin hair.

"I don't see how I got stuck doing the clean-up when I was the one who did the cooking," Connor grumbled as he scraped the metal grill from the barbecue with a steel-wool pad. "Why isn't Grace in here doing this?"

"Because we owe her for looking after Connie," Chelsea said.

"Oh. Then what about Kate or Justin?"

Chelsea shrugged. "They have enough to deal with right now. I think Kate's upset over the whole thing with Justin and his boat. They have no real idea what's going to happen to them when the summer ends. Or even before that. Kate's very preoccupied."

Connor gave her a dubious look. "You and I aren't exactly certain about the future ourselves, are we?"

Chelsea avoided his gaze, concentrating instead on trying to locate Connie's pacifier.

"I mean, Chels, we've been so busy coping with the baby . . . with little Connie there, that we haven't had much time to decide what we're going to do." He attacked a stubborn hot-dog remnant. "We were within seconds of being man and wife."

"I know. I was there." Chelsea was strangely annoyed at the way he was bringing it up. The truth was, she wasn't sure how she felt about that whole thing. In some ways, nothing had changed—Connor was still in the country illegally. He could still be best protected by marrying an American citizen.

But in other ways, so much had changed, starting with the fact that he might have fathered a child with Molly.

"I don't know, Connor," she said wearily. "I guess when I get back from New York, when we don't have a baby to deal with, we'll have to think it all through from the start." She smiled at him, hunched over the sink, trying to rinse the cumbersome grill under the faucet. "At least *that* will be a load off your mind."

"What?" Connor asked. "You mean the baby?"

"Of course I mean the baby. What else have you been whining about for the last week?"

Connor turned off the water and laid the grill down on the counter. His eyes seemed to linger for a moment on the sleeping infant. "Yeah, well, I thought I'd go down to the clinic tomorrow, take Connie along, and settle this matter once and for all."

It took Chelsea a moment to realize what he was saying. "You want to take a blood test? Why? Molly's willing to let you off the hook. You should be thrilled."

Connor wiped his hands on a paper towel. "I am," he said, keeping his eyes averted. "Only . . . I ought to be sure."

"I don't get it," Chelsea said.

Connor rolled his eyes in exasperation. "Look, what if she *is* mine, eh? What if she really is? I can't simply walk away, can I?"

"People do it all the time," Chelsea said in a low voice. "Especially men."

"No, *not* men," Connor said. "Overgrown boys, maybe. Not men. The last thing I want is to be saddled with a kid, but if it's mine, then by God I won't just dump her on Molly."

"What *would* you do?"

Connor stared off into space, thinking. "I suppose I'd at least help pay her way, and Molly's, as much as I was able. See that she was doing all right. Let her know she had a father."

"I don't know what to say," Chelsea admitted. "I assumed you'd be happy to bail out. You've barely paid any attention to Connie, except to complain about her."

Connor frowned at her. "There's a big difference between stepping up and accepting your responsibilities as a man and wanting to change stinking diapers, Chelsea. You can count on me for the one. As to the other, you can count on me to use my every trick to avoid it."

Chelsea came over to him and leaned against his back, wrapping her arms around his warm chest. "You know something," she said, feeling emotion swell in her throat, "I think you're all right."

Connor twisted around until they were face to face. "I think you'd find I'm better than all right," he said with a leering grin, "if you'd only let me demonstrate."

Chelsea banged her forehead against Connor's chest. Typical Connor. He couldn't let a tender moment alone. He couldn't stand the sentimentality of it. It was part of his complex character, his need to always seem like a bad boy. Not for the first time Chelsea wondered if she'd be able to live with it . . . forever.

He kissed her gently. It was one thing he always did with absolute conviction. Chelsea didn't want to mislead him, didn't want to send the signal that she was actually considering his joking suggestion. But at the same time, it was impossible to pull away.

Fortunately—or unfortunately—Connie chose that moment to join the discussion.

Chelsea sighed. "Nice timing," she told the baby. "Okay, Connor, this time you can at least *help* me change the diaper." He made no reply. "Connor?"

She turned around, but Connor had already disappeared.

Marta listened as Alec's breathing grew slower, deeper, and more regular. He lay on his side, his face turned toward her, one muscular arm curled beneath the pillow. His other arm was draped across her stomach. She believed one of his legs was touching hers, but she couldn't be sure.

Moonlight escaped the blinds and colored the carved wood bedposts with silver. A milky beam illuminated Mr. Z, the stuffed pink-striped zebra that perched on her dresser. Her father had laid Mr. Z at her side while she'd been slipping in and out of her coma. He'd bought it for her, he'd said, because it looked so out of place among the mass of tubes, the wires, the IV bags, the electronic monitors. He knew that during those moments when she drifted back to consciousness, she'd be terrified by the machinery that seemed to have taken over her body. He'd wanted her to see something bright and ridiculous. By that point, of course, he had already known what she would not learn for some weeks.

Marta let her eyes wander around the dark room, picking out a detail here and there in the darkness. Her bed, her room, all familiar in every detail, except for this new detail—the man beside her.

She searched her feelings, looking for the revolutionary change she had always somehow expected. Surely from now on nothing would be quite the same. Surely she was different, changed. She was a woman, now, wasn't she?

Marta did feel different. And yet not, too. Like her room, she thought—the same, except for one detail.

Of course, it was a major detail. She smiled at Mr. Z. *I hope you kept your eyes closed*, she thought. She remembered the moments, some awkward, some magical, some funny. Some, she thought, that had threatened to set the room on fire.

She smothered a laugh. Was that smoke she smelled? Because it certainly ought to be.

Suddenly the smile froze on her lips. She sniffed the air.

Wait a minute. That *was* smoke.

"ALEC!"

"AHHH! Is he here?" Alec threw back the covers, then drew them back, then threw them away again. He leapt from the bed, spun around twice, then stopped, staring at Marta. "Where is he?"

Marta didn't have to ask whom Alec was talking about. "It's not that. My dad isn't here. But I think the house is on fire."

Alec breathed a sigh of relief. "Oh, jeez, you almost gave me a heart attack. For the second time tonight," he added.

"Alec, I smell smoke," Marta said calmly.

"Damn. So do I."

"I'll call 911," Marta said. "Why don't you go and take a look. Only, be careful."

Alec ran to the living room while Marta dialed 911. He returned as the call was connected.

"911," the voice in her ear said, sounding bored. "What is the nature of your emergency?"

Marta looked at Alec. "What is the nature of our emergency?"

"The coffee table's on fire!"

"We have a burning coffee table!" Marta said into the phone. Suddenly black smoke billowed into the bedroom through the door Alec had left open. He jumped to close the door.

Marta hung up. "They're on their way!" she said. She gulped hard. For a paraplegic, fire was a special threat.

"I think it was the candle," Alec said.

"Who cares? Let's get out of here!"

"We'll have to go out the window. How high up are we?"

91

"Alec, we're on the ground floor."

"Good. That's good." Alec ran to the window, which was high in the wall but easily large enough to get through. He pushed it open and stared out.

Despite the danger of the moment, Marta couldn't help grinning. "Alec, you don't have anything on."

Alec looked down at himself in alarm. "My clothes are out in the living room!" He glanced desperately toward Marta's closet.

"I don't have anything that would fit you," Marta said. "Forget I mentioned it. Let's bail."

"You aren't exactly dressed for the prom yourself."

Smoke began pouring in under the door. "Look," Marta said, coughing, "we have to get out of here and to hell with modesty."

"Right." Alec jumped toward her and scooped her up in one easy move. Marta held on to her blankets and wrapped them around herself as best she could.

"Mr. Z!" Marta yelled.

"What?"

She pointed. "I have to take Mr. Z."

Alec made a face but carried her to the dresser, where she grabbed the stuffed zebra. She ducked her head as he lifted her through the window. Then, tightening his grip under her shoulders, he released her legs, letting them dangle limply. She could see her toes graze the sparse grass outside. He let her slide through his arms until her legs folded and her rear end hit the ground.

Marta rolled onto her back and quickly pushed herself up into a sitting position. "Alec!" she cried.

"I'm coming," the muffled voice yelled from inside.

"Get out of there!" The distant wail of sirens floated on the cool night wind.

"I'm looking for something!"

"Alec, get out of there right this minute!"

Alec stuck his head out the window and grinned. "Found 'em." He held up two torn, square foil packages. "I didn't want your dad going through the wreckage tomorrow and finding these in the ashes beside your bed."

Marta nodded. "Okay, that *was* good thinking. Now get *out* here!"

Alec climbed through the window, an action hampered somewhat by the fact that he was wearing a pink terry-cloth bathrobe many, many sizes too small for him. He had put it on backward, with the opening at the rear. When he turned, the reason for that fashion choice became obvious. The robe went only about halfway around.

"I suppose this New York thing means you'll

be missing your flying lesson this week," David said. He leaned casually against the porch railing, a position that brought his face exactly level with Grace's.

Grace tightened her grip around his waist. He teased her neck with kisses so sweet and light that she felt herself tremble. "I'll be missing more than that," Grace whispered.

"You mean this week's AA meeting?" David asked innocently.

"That's one thing," Grace admitted. She kissed him slowly, taking her time, making it last.

"Missing work?" David asked when she allowed him to come up for air.

"That's another," Grace agreed. "Only that's not quite what I had in mind." She took his stubbled face in both hands and kissed him again, even longer, even slower, letting herself melt against him.

David's voice was slightly shaky. "Oh, so you'll miss *me*?"

A car driving down the street interrupted Grace's reply. She turned to see a taxi squealing to a stop right alongside the house. The back door opened and out stepped Alec.

Grace took in the reversed pink bathrobe and the angry scowl on Alec's face. He stomped over on bare feet, looked up defiantly at them and placed his fists on his hips. "I need to borrow five bucks to pay the cab," he said.

After a moment of stunned hesitation, David pulled a five-dollar bill from his jeans and handed it down to Alec.

"I'm going to beat the crap out of the first person who laughs," Alec warned.

When he turned around, Grace erupted in amazed, gleeful laughter.

Alec stormed back to the cab, threw the money at the driver, and bent over to lift Marta.

"Oh, man," David groaned, covering his eyes. "I didn't need to see that."

Grace made a back-and-forth gesture with her hand. "I don't know. I've seen worse."

Alec came stomping back over with Marta in his arms. She was wrapped in a soot-stained sheet and holding a pink zebra.

"Grace, David," Marta said, nodding a casual hello.

"Hi, Marta," Grace said as Alec carried her past and into the house.

"So," Grace said to David. "It looks like they had a good date."

NINE

The next morning Connor, Chelsea, and the baby went to the little clinic off the boardwalk. Chelsea and Connor had been there together once before, to have a blood test in preparation for their wedding. That test had shown, among other things, that Chelsea was blood-type A negative and was HIV negative, as well as free of several types of venereal disease. And, since Marta had been there and Marta was a friend, Chelsea had also learned she had a cholesterol level of 220. She should stay away from eggs, butter, and bacon. Of course, Chelsea never ate eggs, bacon, or butter. She'd been on a diet for five of her eighteen years.

During the same test, Connor had learned that he was O positive, that he, too, was free of the usual diseases—although in his case there had been somewhat more reason for concern.

And even though he ate whatever he felt like, including eggs, bacon, and butter, his cholesterol was only 180.

On this trip only Connie gave blood, and then only a small amount, a smear, because no one really thought she had any diseases, and she was much too young to start worrying about cholesterol.

The nurse chatted with them while they waited for the results. She asked them whether they knew if Marta was all right, since she had called in with an excuse that morning, and Marta never missed her shift. An hour later Marta's father had called looking for her, and sounded as if someone were choking him. "We were all wondering if she was okay," the nurse concluded.

Chelsea shrugged. "I talked to our roommate Grace this morning, and she said something about sheets and pink bathrobes, but I didn't really understand her," she said truthfully. "But she was laughing, so I guess Marta's fine."

The door opened and the doctor entered, a youngish guy with prematurely receding hair who wore shorts and a Hawaiian shirt under his lab coat. He stared down at the chart in his hands. "Well, we have the results," he announced.

"Yes?" Connor asked nervously.

"I don't know whether this will be good news to you or bad, not knowing your situation," the doctor said. "And frankly, there are better tests that do this more accurately, but they take four weeks. In general, though, and assuming you have the mother's blood type correct—"

"I called her mum in Ireland," Connor said. "What I told you is what she told me."

Chelsea took a deep breath and held it.

"Let's hear it," Connor said.

"Well, Mr. Riordan, you and the mother test the same blood type. The baby's blood type is B."

"Which means?" Connor demanded.

"In all probability, you are not the baby's father."

Chelsea exhaled and unconsciously tightened her hold on Connie. The baby continued to look around the room, unaware of the momentousness of the occasion.

"She's not mine, then?" Connor asked flatly.

"No."

"No possibility of a mistake?"

"We'd be more certain with DNA testing, but for a fast and dirty answer, no." The doctor smiled uncertainly and glanced at the nurse for reassurance. "Is this good news or bad?"

Connor smiled his crooked grin, committing only half his mouth to the effort. "A bit of both, I suppose."

They didn't speak till they were back out on the boardwalk. The sun was still mild this early in the day, only a quarter of the way up. The surfers who'd been riding the waves since five and six in the morning were packing it in, and the tourist sunbathers were starting to set out their blankets and beach towels. Lifeguards were arriving at their posts, and shops were opening, setting out their racks of postcards and T-shirts.

"Well," Chelsea said as they reached the turnoff for home, "I guess I'll get Connie to her baby-sitter. You'd better get to work."

Connor made a face, halfway between agreement and annoyance. Then he stuck out his hands. "I'll carry her on back. The job will live without me for another half hour."

Chelsea started to laugh, it was so unexpected. She began to point out that he had never before wanted to carry the baby, but she stopped herself. She handed the baby to Connor, and with a pat on his shoulder, went off down the boardwalk to pick up her cameras and start her day's work.

The knock on the door that morning sounded perfectly innocent. Only when Alec went to answer it and saw who was standing on his porch did he realize the danger he was in.

Luis set the wheelchair down beside the door and smiled a smile that would have frozen a square mile of desert.

"I brought this by," Luis said. "I thought Marta might need it."

Alec opened the door and tried to start his heart again. Marta was sitting on the couch, sipping a cup of coffee. She was wearing a robe she'd borrowed from Grace.

"Daddy," she said with what seemed to Alec like superhuman calm. "You're back early. I didn't expect you home till this afternoon."

"I know. I guess it's a surprise for you," Luis said. "But then, I found my own surprise this morning. I have to admit, I *was* surprised."

"Um, about that—" Alec began.

"There I am," Luis said, stepping to the middle of the room. "Getting home after a long drive, thinking to myself, I have the rest of the day off, maybe I'll take it easy. Maybe I'll putter around the house."

Alec winced. He looked at Marta, but she actually appeared a little bored.

"Then I see that Marta's wheelchair is by the front door. I am surprised by this. I wonder how this has happened." He turned to Alec. "I enjoy a good mystery, don't you?"

"Luis . . . Mr. Salgado . . ."

"But that's nothing. The real mystery is not *Why is Marta's wheelchair by the front door?* Oh, no. The real mystery is *Where is the damned door?*"

Alec jumped back several feet as Luis's pent-up rage boiled over. But instantly Luis grew calm again.

"I step inside," he continued, "and what do I see? Blackness." He made a dramatic gesture and lowered his voice. "Blackness. My couch is . . . *black*. My television . . . *black*. My walls . . . *black*. Everything is black. And of course," he added as an afterthought, "very, very wet."

"The fire department—" Alec began. "I mean, you know, they had to put the fire out."

"Yes, they explained that to me when I called them up and asked them *what in hell had happened*."

"Okay, there was a fire," Alec said.

"Really, Daniels? There was a fire? Was there really?" Luis sighed heavily. "The fireman assured me that no one had been hurt. My daughter was fine. And I was so relieved. What a load off my mind. Then, he told me my *son* was all right too! My *son*, who he described as big and blond. Then this fireman began to giggle. He began to laugh so hard he had to hang up."

"I didn't want to complicate things, that's why I said I was your son," Alec admitted. He looked at Marta. "Is he going to hurt me?"

Marta shook her head. "Not yet. Soon."

"Then I checked with my neighbors, all of whom told the same story of a big, blond boy who came knocking at their doors last night to warn them. Fortunately, the fire did not spread to any of their apartments. So, I guess everyone was lucky." Luis let his voice drop to a weary calm. "And after all, we have insurance to pay for everything, so hey, no big deal."

Alec could hardly believe his ears. Was Luis really letting this go?

"There is one little thing I don't understand, Daniels," Luis went on. "All the neighbors, they all agreed on one thing. The big blond guy? He was wearing a pink bathrobe. Backward." He stepped closer, almost standing on his toes to thrust his face into Alec's. "And under the robe? Nothing."

A hundred explanations raced through Alec's mind. Each dumber than the one before.

"Where were your clothes, Daniels?" Luis demanded, his voice menacing.

"On fire?" Alec suggested. He was strangely fascinated by the way the veins in Luis's forehead were standing out. Not to mention the way Luis was drawing back his fist and—

"Daddy!" Marta snapped sharply. "His clothes were in the living room."

"You're a dead man," Luis said.

"So were mine," Marta added. This time her voice was more subdued.

"No, death is too good, too easy. You molest my daughter and burn down my home!"

"Alec, maybe you should step outside for a minute while I talk to my father alone," Marta suggested. "I think he's ready to blow."

But Alec surprised himself by shaking his head. "I can handle this," he said.

Suddenly Luis's right hand shot toward Alec's throat. Alec caught the wrist, stopping his fingers centimeters from their goal. He had expected Luis to be strong, but Alec was much larger, and no weakling. He was amazed when Luis's fingers inched forward.

"Daddy! Alec! Both of you, stop being such men."

Luis's fingers moved closer. It was impossible. He was twenty years older and fifty pounds lighter.

"NOW!" Marta rapped out the word.

Luis slowly drew back. Alec released his wrist but kept a wary eye on him.

"Daddy, I think it's time we had a talk," Marta said. "Alec, if you wouldn't mind."

Alec nodded. He'd stood up to Luis, but there was such a thing as pushing it too far.

He headed for the porch and sank down onto the top step. Justin was just leaving the boathouse on his way to work, whistling contentedly.

"Hey, what's with you, man?" he called.

Alec stared bleakly at him. "I burned up Luis's apartment."

"You burned up our boss's apartment," Justin repeated. "Okay. Any particular reason?"

Alec sighed. "I was there with Marta. You know, sort of late. Very late."

Justin's face fell. "Are you telling me you slept with Luis's daughter and then, as if that weren't quite enough, you burned his place up?"

"He's in there now," Alec said glumly, jerking his thumb toward the house.

"I don't know you, I've never met you, stay away from me. You are clearly insane," Justin said. "Please don't ever come near me again. I wouldn't want to be killed as an innocent bystander."

"He tried to choke me!" Alec said, suddenly indignant.

"He *tried*? And you're still alive?"

"He's amazingly strong for a little guy."

"No kidding. Don't you know how he got away from that shark?" Justin asked, glancing nervously toward the door. "He pried open its jaws with his bare hands. A shark that could chew through a Volkswagen. Good-bye, you poor dumb sucker. It was nice knowing you." He took off at a trot.

A moment later, the door opened. Luis stepped out. Alec got wearily to his feet, preparing to do what he could and hoping his injuries wouldn't be life-threatening.

But to Alec's amazement, Luis simply brushed past him and headed away in the same direction Justin had gone.

He let out a huge sigh of relief, then realized Marta was in the doorway, sitting in her wheelchair. "What did you say to him?" Alec demanded, almost laughing with relief.

Marta looked thoughtful. "I told him I was in love with you. And I said that while we look for a new apartment, I thought I'd take you up on your offer to stay here for a day or two."

"And he accepted that?" Alec asked.

Marta bit her lip. It was a rare moment, Alec realized. For once Marta looked uncertain. "I don't know," she admitted. "He listened. And then, he seemed to . . . to pull away from me. I think it was the first time he'd ever heard me say I loved anyone but him. I think maybe it made him a little sad."

Alec whistled under his breath. Luis sad? Better sad than furious, he supposed.

"He's gone off to find a new place," Marta said.

"Where's he going to stay till then?" Alec asked.

Marta shrugged. "You said the house would be almost empty for the next few days, what with Kate, Chelsea, and Grace off with the baby, and Justin on his boat. So . . ."

"You didn't," Alec cried. "He's not staying here. With us?"

"He seemed so sad, I thought maybe the idea of having you close by, you know, so you two can get to know each other for a few days, would cheer him up." Marta smiled. "It did."

"Are you going to keep working all night?" Kate asked in frustration, calling down to Justin from the loft.

Justin looked up at her from the deck of his boat. For several hours he'd been checking the boat's supplies against a list on a clipboard. When something wasn't quite right, he immediately took care of the problem before going on to the next item.

"I'm almost done," he said distractedly. Then he smiled. "Sorry. It's my first major trip out, and I don't want anything to go wrong."

Kate shook her head and came down the stairs. "What could go wrong?" she asked. "You're going off into the ocean on a tiny little boat about the size of two cars. What could possibly go wrong?"

Justin grinned. "It's not such a tiny boat," he pointed out. "You know, Columbus's boats were only two to three times as long."

"Yeah, two to three times," Kate repeated.

"But this boat is far, far safer than those old caravels. Much stronger construction, infinitely stronger sails, a much more sophisticated mast and rigging. I mean, it's like comparing a Model T to a brand-new Mercedes." He put down the clipboard and took her hand as she stepped aboard. "Not to mention a few other minor differences, like for example, Columbus didn't know where he was going, or really where he was. Me, I punch a button and satellites up in orbit tell me exactly where I am within a couple of feet. And if I get in trouble, I have a radio to call up the Coast Guard and get help. Also, I'm pretty sure Columbus didn't have a CD player."

"So it's perfectly safe?" Kate asked, half mocking, half serious.

"Perfectly? No." Justin picked up his clipboard again. "But then, driving to New York in a beat-up old convertible isn't perfectly safe, either, is it? In fact," he said with a scowl, "I should be the one worrying about you. There are no muggers in the ocean."

"There are no forty-foot waves in Manhattan."

Justin nodded. "So, you girls ready for the big road trip?" He held up his clipboard. "Do you all have an official trip clipboard?"

"I think we're ready," Kate said. "Luis is using my room and Marta's sleeping in the dining room, which means Alec is jumping at every strange noise he hears. Looks like the next couple of days are going to be a good time to be out of the house." She paused. "You know, I think Grace is the most excited by this whole trip, although she's acting very cool about it."

"As long as I've known her, she's been hot to travel." Justin peered down through the hatch and made a check mark on his list. "You know. See the world, get out of Ocean City."

"Are you going to miss me?" Kate asked. She regretted it immediately. It was stupid thing to ask. After all, Justin had practically begged her to go with him.

He looked at her seriously, his eyes wary. "Of course I will. There's no doubt about that. The question is whether you'll miss me."

"Why would you say that?" Kate asked. "Of course I'll miss you."

"I wish you were going with me, so I could show you how great it can be," Justin said softly. "Visiting your college this way . . ." He shrugged self-consciously. "Well, to me it almost feels like you're going to visit another guy. I guess I'm afraid you're going to fall in love, Kate."

"You're selling yourself short, Justin," she argued. "It's you I'm in love with, not some collection of buildings."

He held her gaze until she felt uncomfortable and looked away. Then he nodded. "I guess I'll have to hope your love for me is strong enough."

Kate started to answer, then realized that there was nothing she could say that would reassure him. "Well," she said brightly, "I'm all packed, and we're hoping to get an early start, so I guess I'll try to get to sleep. Are you coming?"

Justin smiled wistfully. "I'll be right up," he said. "I'll be done here in a minute."

Kate walked back to the stairs, feeling troubled. Halfway up, she stopped. "I *do* love you, Justin," she whispered.

Justin said nothing, ducking his head to enter the cabin and disappearing from view.

Probably, Kate thought, he hadn't heard her. Probably.

TEN

Grace woke up sobbing. Fortunately, she'd pulled the pillow tight against her face in her sleep. She doubted if anyone in the house had heard her. That was a relief. The dream—the memory, actually—was humiliating enough.

She flung the pillow away and disentangled herself from the damp sheets that had wrapped themselves around her legs.

She needed a drink. The dreams had drained away the thin veneer of self-confidence she'd only begun to restore. Each time she had one, it reminded her that she wasn't the person she pretended to be.

She was weak. Desperately weak. She knew now that the cool, in-control person she'd always thought she saw in the mirror was a farce. She couldn't pretend to be strong when she knew the truth. She couldn't pretend to be proud. Not anymore. Not ever again.

How do you tell yourself you're strong and proud and admirable, when you know in your soul that you're a slave to a bottle of alcohol? How do you manage to rebuild your pride, when each day the memory of humiliation remains so strong?

"You don't," Grace whispered to the dark. No, you admit the truth—that you're weak. That you're a slave. And you accept it, and live with it.

Why try to stay sober? For what? To fool the world into believing she was all right when she knew that she wasn't, not really?

Grace climbed out of bed. She wanted a drink. *Tell the truth*, she dared herself. *You want several drinks. You want dozens of drinks. You want gallons of it, till you can't walk or think or remember. That's the truth, Grace. That's the truth, you sickening drunk.*

She pulled on a pair of jeans and slipped on a light cotton sweater. Then she thought better of it and replaced the sweater with a silk blouse. *Yes*, she thought bitterly, *that silk blouse.* Much better.

The living room was dark, and Grace crept across the wood floor on bare feet, holding her sandals in one hand, her purse in the other.

"Is someone there?" a sleepy voice asked.

Grace froze in panic. Then she remembered—Marta was sleeping on a cot in the dining room. "It's only me," Grace whispered. "Sorry I woke you."

The night air was chilly, freshened by a wet

breeze that felt like some fugitive from autumn. Grace checked her watch. The dials showed one twenty-five. Perfect. It was almost closing time, and the bars would be emptying out of all the amateurs, all the hopeful singles, leaving behind the serious drinkers, the ones who would never leave until the last call.

She walked in broad, easy strides toward the boardwalk. Suddenly she felt like laughing aloud. It was liberating. She was free! She was doing exactly what she wanted to do, what she needed to do, and to hell with the rest of the human race.

She climbed the wooden steps from the street to the boardwalk. The boards were definitely closing down. The souvenir shops, family restaurants, and video arcades were all dark, hidden behind steel mesh gates. Only the bars were still open.

The blue neon sign jutting out over the door to Petie's was still lit. Grace sauntered toward the blue light.

As soon as she pushed open the swinging door, the smell hit her. Beer, mostly. Bitter and sour-smelling. And the sweeter smells of whiskey, the root-beer smell of bourbon, the pepper of scotch. Lime and lemon peel and cherries. And then there were the sounds—a jukebox that was all bass, the clink of ice, the murmur of conversation, the ringing of the cash register.

Yes, it was all there, the way she remembered

it. Only the howling wind of the hurricane was missing.

There were half a dozen drunks at the long mahogany bar, curled around their drinks, guarding them as if someone might try to steal them. They stared into space, taking each swallow at a measured, regular pace, making it last.

The stage where Petie held his wet T-shirt contests was dark. The people who drank here this late didn't come for the entertainment.

Then Grace saw him, waddling behind the bar, a cigarette in his mouth. His shrewd little eyes were fixed on an old man who was staggering in the direction of the rest room.

Grace felt her insides lurch. She struggled to breathe. She had to force herself forward, riding past a wave of nausea.

She sat down at the bar. Petie's eyes locked onto her. A smirk formed on his lips. He let her sit for several minutes before sidling over.

"Hey, sweet thing."

Grace nodded, not trusting her voice.

"Back to finish what we started?"

"I want a drink. Scotch. Neat."

The smirk grew. "Of course you do, sweet thing. One to get you started, anyway. Later . . . well, we'll see about later when it gets later."

He pulled a bottle from the shelf behind him and a glass from beneath the bar. "As I remember it, you had good taste for a woman as young

112

as yourself," he said, pouring the pale golden liquid. He leered at her blouse. "Not the only good thing about you, either."

Grace stared at the full, brimming glass. The tangy, sharp aroma filled her nose. She realized she was salivating in anticipation of the taste, the burning feel as it slid down her throat.

She bit her lip and reached for the glass as Petie gave a satisfied nod, knowing what she was, knowing the desperate thirst that raged in her. Grace raised the glass to within an inch of her lips. She focused her gaze on Petie, willing herself to meet his eyes.

"You're . . ." Her throat clutched up and she had to swallow before starting again. "You're a vile, disgusting pig of a man," Grace said, carefully enunciating each word.

Petie's eyes went wide in surprise. Grace tossed the drink in his face. He staggered back, clawing at his eyes.

Grace climbed down from the barstool and headed across the room. All eyes were on her. Only when she reached the door did she realize she was still holding the empty glass. And only then did her calm desert her.

A feeling, more powerful than she had ever felt before in her life, welled up inside her. Her hands trembled. Her lips quivered. It seemed the very air around her had turned red as blood.

"You bitch!" Petie roared.

Grace spun and with one fluid movement launched the glass through the air. It hit him in the lower lip. She realized she was screaming at him, her fists clenched in rage. She turned blindly and shoved open the door, still electric with pent-up fury.

"Nobody does that to me!"

Grace spun around as a thrill of fear shot through her. He had followed her outside.

Petie loomed in the doorway, teeth bared, eyes wild. "You'll pay for this!" he said, touching the bloody split in his lip. He charged her like a mad bear.

Then, before Grace could even react, Petie was on the ground, slammed against the boards. A dark figure stood over him.

"Stay down there, you piece of crap, because I swear if you stand up I'll kill you." David knelt, placing his knee on Petie's throat. His voice was unnaturally calm. "Now apologize to the young lady."

"For what—" Petie began, but his protest ended in a strangling sound. He gasped and sucked at air. "Okay, okay. I apologize."

"Good," David said cheerfully, rising to his feet. "This time you get to apologize. Next time, I perform some surgery on you. Think about it. It means exactly what you think it means."

Petie crawled back to the safety of his bar. David walked over to Grace, who was hugging herself for warmth in the chill ocean air.

"That was about the stupidest thing you could possibly have done, Grace," he said angrily. "You do realize that, don't you? Stupid. Idiotic. Lunatic."

Grace nodded. She was shaking violently.

"Good. As long as we're clear on that." David took her in his arms, sharing his warmth with her. He broke out in a grin. "You're absolutely the best, Grace."

"How did you—?"

"Marta called me," David explained. "She was worried."

"How did you know where to look?"

"Oh, I knew. I knew you'd come here."

"But I wasn't sure *why* I was coming here, David," Grace admitted. "I wanted a drink so badly. And I wasn't really sure until he poured me that drink. Then I knew."

David smiled. "I had no doubt."

Suddenly Grace smiled, too. She had to bite her lip to keep from laughing in sheer relief. "Damn," she said. "I did it."

"Yeah, you did. And in memorable style too. But then, you always have had a certain flair, Racy Grace." David draped his arm around her shoulder. "Come on, I'll walk you home."

"No." Grace shook her head. She grazed his lips with a kiss. "How about if I walk you home instead?"

*　　*　　*

The big red convertible sat chugging softly, sending out a cloud of steam as its hot exhaust hit the damp, chilly morning air. Kate lugged her suitcase down the front porch steps, annoyed that it kept banging against her bare leg. She'd get a bruise if she had to carry it much farther.

She set it down and opened the trunk. The suitcase fit, with plenty of room left over. That was a good thing, since Chelsea would probably pack everything she owned, not to mention all the baby paraphernalia. And Grace . . . well, Grace had been known to change clothes three times before breakfast.

Speaking of which. Where *was* Grace?

Chelsea stumbled down the stairs, a suitcase in one hand and a big bag of diapers, lotions, wipes, bottles, and bibs in the other.

Kate heard a hammering sound from the direction of the water. Justin had moved the boat out of the boathouse and tethered it to the end of their dock. Connor was helping Justin raise the mast and secure it in place. It was strange. She'd never seen the stern before, where he had painted *J's Boat.* It had always been bow first in the boathouse. Justin's Boat. She hadn't really realized it . . . *she* . . . had a name.

"Have you seen Grace?" Chelsea asked as she piled her stuff on top of Kate's.

"No, I'm starting to wonder where she is," Kate

said anxiously. She stared back at Justin's boat. He was only going on a two-day trip along the coast, but to both of them it symbolized so much more.

"I looked in her room," Chelsea said. "Her bags are packed and her bed's been slept in."

Kate winced. She knew what Chelsea was thinking. The same thought had already crossed Kate's mind. Had Grace fallen off the wagon? Was she on another bender? Kate glanced at her watch. Where else would Grace be at seven fifteen A.M.?

Down the street she noticed two runners, one large young man, one smaller and more wiry. Both wore Beach Patrol T-shirts.

They reached the car, and Alec waved Luis on wearily. "Go ahead, you can hit the shower first," he gasped. As soon as Luis was inside, Alec collapsed against the car. "He's trying to kill me. Only he's using subtle means."

"You guys went running?" Chelsea asked. "I didn't even see you go out."

"That's because we left at *five thirty*," Alec rasped. "Almost two hours, and it's not like the guy takes it easy, either."

"Why'd you go running with him?" Kate asked.

"Because he woke me up and *told* me we were going for a run. I thought, okay, he's ready to bond. We'll do a couple miles, we'll become little work-out buddies." He scowled. "If I'm dead by the time you girls get back, you'll know why."

Alec staggered toward the house, using his

hands to help push himself up the stairs.

"So where's Grace?" Chelsea demanded. "We're ready. What are we going to do?"

"You get the baby ready," Kate said. "If Grace isn't here in ten minutes, we write her off." She paused, her annoyance overtaken by worry. "Okay, we don't write her off. If she isn't here in ten minutes, we call David. And maybe her brother. Then we have another cup of coffee and worry some more."

"And then?"

"Then we worry about what to do next."

While Chelsea went to retrieve Connie, Connor and Justin crossed the lawn to join Kate. "You girls ready to go?" Connor asked as they drew near.

"Grace seems to be missing," Kate said.

Justin shook his head. "Man, I hope this isn't what you think it is."

"I don't think anything," Kate lied. She put on a calm smile. "So are you all set?"

Justin snapped a salute. "All squared away and ready to shove off for sea trials."

"Have you battened down the hatches?"

"Hatches battened," he said with a grin. "How's your heap?"

"I'm letting it warm up plenty so we won't have to do the usual early-morning stall-at-every-stop routine," Kate said. "And yes, Dad, I checked the oil."

Chelsea came out of the house, letting the door swing shut behind her. She held the baby, bundled in her little carrier. "Okay," she said. "We're all set. I'd really like to get started while Connie's still asleep."

Connor pulled the baby's blanket aside gently to reveal her rosy face. "Nice knowing you, Connie girl," he said softly. He turned away abruptly, brushing his hand over his face.

An instant later Kate noticed the sound of a deep-throated engine, much louder than the sullen rumble from her car. A motorcycle turned down their street and slowed to a stop. David pulled off his helmet and gave a casual wave as Grace hopped off the back of the Harley. She pulled off her own helmet and handed it to David. Then, while both his hands were full, she gave him a quick kiss and flashed a smile at Kate and Chelsea.

David pushed his helmet back on his head and roared off.

"We weren't sure you were coming," Kate remarked.

Grace looked both tired and elated. "Wouldn't miss this trip for anything," she said breezily. "Let me grab my bags from inside."

Kate and Chelsea exchanged a look. "I guess we know what we'll be talking about on the way there," Chelsea remarked.

Kate made her farewell to Justin as brief as she

could. Justin seemed to be thinking the same thing.

Grace returned with her bags in tow. She stuck them in the overstuffed trunk and promptly made herself comfortable in the passenger seat, using a box of Pampers as a pillow. Chelsea strapped the baby into the child seat in the back and climbed in beside her. Connor bent over to kiss her good-bye.

"Well, I guess I'll see you in a couple days," Justin told Kate.

Kate kissed him lightly on the mouth. "Be careful out there."

"Piece of cake," Justin said. "*You* be careful."

"Yeah, yeah, yeah, can we get going here?" Grace complained.

"Bye," Kate said. She climbed in behind the wheel and drove off down the street. At the corner, she glanced in her rearview mirror. Justin was still standing there, watching her.

She sighed and pulled onto the main drag, turning right toward the bridge. As she passed along the nearly empty street, she spotted a mailbox and pulled up beside it.

"What, are we there already?" Grace mumbled, opening one eye.

"Yes, it was a very quick drive." Kate reached into her purse and pulled out the three letters she'd stashed there. One to her parents. One to a mail-order company for some clothes. And the letter of Chelsea's she'd picked up the day before yesterday. She handed them to Grace. "Stick these in, would you?"

"Okay, but I get to sleep the rest of the way," Grace said. "I've been up all night."

"Stop bragging," Chelsea teased.

"One of those was yours, Chels," Kate said.

"What?" Chelsea asked distractedly. She was trying to tuck an extra blanket in around the sleeping Connie. "What's mine?"

"Never mind," Kate said.

ELEVEN

Justin cast off the bowline, raced back to cast off the stern line, and pushed at the edge of the dock with his foot. The boat drifted a few feet out into the bay, clearing the boathouse and the dock. The slight current caught the bow and turned the boat in the wrong direction, but Justin was already busy hoisting the mainsail to take advantage of the fresh offshore breeze.

The sail flapped idly, like someone shaking out a blanket. Then it caught the wind, filled, and pushed the boat several degrees onto its side. Mooch leapt to the bow excitedly, ears flapping, tongue hanging out as if he were tasting the breeze.

"This is it, guy," Justin said. He took the tiller in one hand and began the slow process of tacking toward the inlet. It would be easier to fire up the engine and power his way out of the bay, but this trip was not about what was easy. This trip was to test all the equipment. And the most important piece of equipment on the boat was him.

Justin fastened his safety line, the nylon rope that would keep him attached to his boat in the event he fell or was knocked overboard. Then he poured himself a cup of steaming coffee from his gray metal thermos.

It took twenty minutes to reach the bridge. Justin figured Kate and the girls had crossed it ten minutes earlier. He wondered if they'd been able to see him, fighting his way upwind. He sounded his Klaxon. It took ten minutes before the bridge was raised and he and a big cabin cruiser behind him could pass through. It took another twenty minutes to reach the inlet and fight the stronger current there that seemed determined to keep him from the ocean.

But at last he cleared the inlet and could let the boat run before the wind. The rising sun drew a line of gold across the calm water. Ahead were clear skies, adorned here and there with a puffball of cloud. A small wave smacked the side of the boat and blew a shower of spray over him.

Justin laughed happily. If only Kate had come. She'd have seen. She'd have understood.

The wind was at his back, the sky was clear, no storm threatened. It was a perfect day for sailing, a perfect day. The beach of Ocean City reeled past on his port side as the wind blew him north by northeast along the coast. He and

Kate were traveling in much the same direction, he realized wistfully. Only with utterly different destinations.

"I think it's going to land right on the highway," Kate said nervously.

"Watch the road, Kate," Chelsea advised from the backseat.

"Who cares about cars? That jet is going to land right on top of us."

"No it's not," Grace said calmly. "And if it does, it will all be over so quickly, you won't have time to worry."

"I have time to worry right now," Kate said, glancing every second and a half at the 747 that was dropping toward them.

"It's only a . . ."

Grace's answer was swallowed in the ear-splitting roar of the jet as it passed overhead so closely that she was certain she could see the individual treads on the landing wheels. As soon as it passed, the noise of the jet gave way to the screech of the baby. Connie had spent at least half the five-hour trip screeching.

Fortunately, between memories of last night with David and a building sense of excitement about what lay ahead, Grace was feeling relatively mellow. Or perhaps she was too tired not to be mellow. She'd hoped to sleep on the way up, but Connie had killed that plan.

"Okay, there are only like three airports on this map," Chelsea said, refolding the road map. "That was definitely an airport we passed back there. Which means we are either right where we should be, or we've driven past Manhattan and are on our way to someplace that's off the edge of the map."

"Hey, sign says Lincoln Tunnel, 495," Grace pointed out. "Isn't that what we want?"

"Should we put the top up?" Kate wondered. "I mean, before we get into the city? You know, to be safe."

"Great idea," Grace agreed. "Where do you propose we pull over to do that? If we even slow down, we're going to have about twenty-five tractor trailers roll right over us."

"Tunnel, follow the tunnel," Chelsea said. "Tunnels are good. Come on, Connie, good baby, chill out, all right?"

The baby actually quieted. Grace turned in the seat to peer at Chelsea over the top of her shades. "Chill out?"

"It worked, didn't it?"

The traffic slowed to a crawl as they approached the tunnel entrance. "Are they kidding? Another toll?" Kate complained. "Like the New Jersey Turnpike wasn't bad enough? Now they want four bucks to go through a tunnel?"

"Look, you two haven't been back here taking care of a baby," Chelsea pointed out. "If you had,

125

you'd be ready to spend whatever it costs to get to where Molly is staying. Right now—although Connie certainly is a sweet baby—I'd give several major body parts in exchange for handing her over to her real mommy."

"Aw, what's happened to your nurturing instincts?" Grace said.

"Used up," Chelsea snapped. "Burned out. I'll tell you something—anyone who thinks raising a baby is fun ought to try it for a week."

"Well, look at it from the kid's point of view," Grace offered. "Twenty years from now she'll probably be sitting in some psychiatrist's office saying, 'But doctor, I'm sure I have this strange memory of a time when my mother was black.'"

"Is it just me or does the air stink?" Kate wondered. "I mean, as opposed to baby-stink."

"Of course the air stinks. It's New York," Grace said. "Try to get into the spirit of things, Kate. We're on an adventure." Of course, the grimy tiled walls of the tunnel around them didn't seem like the best start to an adventure. "I wonder if they maintain this thing. I mean, billions of gallons of river water waiting for a break to rush in . . ."

"Have I mentioned I have a touch of claustrophobia?" Kate said. "Sometimes, if I'm in a confined area, you know, like a *tunnel*, I lose it totally. Go nuts, screaming and tearing my hair and babbling incoherently."

"Very funny," Chelsea said from the backseat.

"That's not claustrophobia," Grace said. "It's P.M.S."

The tunnel seemed to go on forever, a noisy, smoky, choking purgatory. But then, for Grace, the reward appeared. They rose from the tunnel into a forest of tall buildings that seemed to push away the sky. Any one of them held more people on a busy day than the entire off-season population of Ocean City.

"New York," Grace whispered. "I'm actually in New York City."

"You know, if you can make it here, you can make it anywhere," Chelsea said, grinning.

"It's the city that never sleeps," Kate added. "Of course, that's because they have to lie awake all night clutching guns in case a crazed crackhead tries to break in and rob them."

"This is so cool," Grace said.

"Yeah, it is, isn't it?" Kate agreed.

"Look at this. Every kind of human being on planet Earth is on these streets. Every race, every religion, every size and shape. The whole sociological and economic and political spectrum. Everything from small-town Iowa to . . . to Vladivostok."

"Vladivostok?" Chelsea echoed.

"Not to mention the entire psychological spectrum," Kate added. "From mildly neurotic to disturbed to machete-swinging psycho."

"This is it," Grace went on. "This is the center of all human civilization. This is the heart of American culture."

"Stop, you're depressing me," Chelsea said.

Suddenly a yellow cab went careening around them, horn blaring. A raised middle finger waved from the window.

"Speaking of civilization," Chelsea said.

"What did I do?" Kate asked.

"Nothing," Chelsea said. "You were driving normally."

"Well, that puts you in the minority, doesn't it?" Grace observed. "I think you're supposed to yell back. Toughen up, kids. You're the ones who are going to be spending the next four years here. You can't let people flip you off and drive away unflipped. An eye for an eye and a finger for a finger. I thought you knew your way around."

"All we've really seen is the school," Kate admitted. "We flew in and Chelsea's dad took us around in a limo. Mostly we saw the campus and the hotel."

"They had a great brunch," Chelsea recalled.

They stopped at a red light and Kate rubbed her eyes with the heels of her hand.

"Tired, huh?" Grace asked sympathetically.

"You can drive when we go back," Kate said.

Just then there was a loud bang on the hood of the car. Grace looked up in surprise to see a middle-aged man, a cigar poking from his face, slam his hand down on the hood again.

"Whaddaya doin', lady? This a freakin' cross-walk. People gotta walk here!"

Kate gripped the wheel and gulped. "Ignore him."

"Let me handle this," Grace said. She sat up higher in her seat. "Hey, you want to walk, walk. You got plenty of room," she yelled.

"You're in the damn crosswalk!"

"What are you wasting my time for? Go around. The light's going to change and we'll run you down."

"Run *me* down!"

"That's right, so move it, old man. You have maybe ten seconds. Nine. Eight."

"Screw you!"

"No, screw you," Grace replied. "Seven, six."

"Ahh," the man waved his hand in angry dismissal and continued across the street.

"See," Grace said, "wherever you go, you have to learn the local language."

Kate looked at her and shook her head. "You want to tell me what that was all about?"

"David. He's from here. He said his best advice for surviving New York was 'Walk fast, avoid eye contact, and don't take any crap.'"

"Oh, so *that's* what you were doing all last night? Getting travel advice from David?" Chelsea laughed.

Grace raised her eyebrow. "That's part of

129

what I was getting from David," she said coyly. She paused, waiting for Chelsea's groan. "That, plus the names of a couple of good delis."

A cab raced past them as they started away from the light. The driver honked his horn and yelled something that came out only as a blur of sound.

"All together now," Grace said.

The three girls from Ocean City raised their right hands in identical middle-finger salutes.

"All right!" Grace said. "Now we're ready for New York."

TWELVE

"Eight bucks to park the car for an hour?" Kate demanded. "I told you we should've kept looking for a parking place."

"Kate," Chelsea said wearily as they walked along the street, "there are no parking places. We looked. Remember? We looked for an hour. The nearest free parking place is in Vermont." She shifted Connie from her left hip to her right. Kate had volunteered to carry the baby's things. Grace was walking several paces ahead, weirdly alert and animated. She'd been like that ever since they'd arrived.

"This is the place," Grace called as she came to a stop in front of an apartment building.

"About time," Chelsea grumbled. "My arm is going numb." She twisted her head to look at the baby in her carrier. "It's a good thing you're not any heavier."

They gave a very abbreviated explanation of their mission to the uniformed doorman and were allowed into the lobby. It was small, but walled with pink marble. The elevator door was polished brass.

"Kind of looks like the Ocean City Grand," Grace remarked.

The elevator to the ninth floor was slow, but they passed the time in silence. Chelsea felt tired. More than that, she was beginning to feel strangely depressed.

They exited and quickly found the door. Kate sent Chelsea a look. "You ready?"

"Why wouldn't I be?" Chelsea answered crankily. Then she answered her own question. "I'm only taking the baby I've kind of gotten used to and handing her over to the woman who broke up my wedding. Why wouldn't I be ready?" With her free hand she knocked on the door.

Molly answered it. She was wearing an expensive-looking gray silk blouse and linen skirt. Her thin blond hair had been cut into a neat chin-length bob. She looked at Chelsea without expression, then dropped her eyes to the baby.

"Oh, my little Connie darling," she cried.

Connie was gone from her arms before Chelsea had time to think about it. Molly whisked her across a tastefully decorated room, twirling the baby in the air, showing no signs of the twisted ankle she'd told Connor about. Chelsea felt Kate's hand find hers and give a comforting squeeze.

An elegant woman who looked about the same age as Chelsea's mother appeared. She took Chelsea's arm, drawing her inside. Kate and Grace fell in behind them.

"Please come in, won't you? I'm Fiona Dane, Molly's aunt." She smiled a little uncertainly. The Irish accent was still present, but subdued. Her clothes were conservative but not frumpy. Her hair was dark and touched faintly with gray. "Please call me Fiona."

"Hi, I'm Chelsea Lennox. These are my friends, Kate Quinn and Grace Caywood."

"My husband, Gerald," Fiona said, indicating a balding man who rose to shake their hands. He was wearing a sports coat and pressed slacks, and looked like the kind of man who never dressed any more casually than that.

"Good to meet you, girls," he said. He spoke with a southern accent, definitely American, Chelsea realized. The realization made her smile. Well, well, she thought. Perhaps Fiona had married Gerald to stay in the country, like she and Connor had considered doing.

"We're sorry we're late," Kate said. "Traffic and parking and so on." She set her bag of baby supplies on the floor.

Chelsea pointed to the bag. "We have all the stuff Molly left with us, plus, you know, a couple things that Connie seems to like." She took a deep breath and glanced up at Molly, who was still parading around the room, making a show of talking to the child she'd abandoned a week earlier.

"You're the one who's marrying Connor, then?" Fiona asked gently.

Chelsea nodded. For some reason, probably lack of sleep, she was feeling terribly sad. She felt like crying, although that would have been a little ridiculous. She ought to be thrilled. She was free again.

"You know, I knew Connor back in Ireland," Fiona said. "Of course, he was a little boy when I knew him, no more than five or six. Tell me, is he still a charmer?"

Chelsea smiled reluctantly. "I guess you could say that."

"I suppose he's grown up all tall and handsome."

Chelsea nodded. Grace made a back-and-forth gesture with her hand.

"Please, won't you have a cup of tea or coffee with us?" Fiona asked.

"I don't think so," Chelsea said. "You know, we have to go find our hotel."

"Yes, well, speaking of that." Fiona opened the drawer of a small table by the door. She took out a buff-colored envelope and handed it to Chelsea. "All this must have cost you quite a bit."

"You don't have to do that," Chelsea protested,

pushing the envelope away. "I mean, it was, you know, kind of fun." To her annoyance, her voice broke a little. "She's a good baby. And I'm glad she can be back with her mother."

Fiona shot a glance in Molly's direction and then back at Chelsea. "Don't worry about little Connie," she said in a low voice. "Gerald and I never had children of our own. We'll see she has a good life. And the Moynihans, Tim's parents, they're good people. Little Connie won't lack for love and attention. We'll have her spoiled rotten in no time."

Chelsea shrugged and swallowed hard.

"Even though Molly doesn't seem to have the sense to thank you for what you've done, my husband and I certainly do. Now take this and don't argue," Fiona said, handing the envelope to Grace this time. "Gerald has more money than he knows what to do with. Besides, New York is such an expensive city."

"Eight bucks to park," Kate said by way of agreement.

"A hundred dollars a night for a room at the West Side Grand, and that's *with* the discount I get for working at the Ocean City Grand," Grace added.

Fiona gave Chelsea a little kiss on the cheek. "Thank you again, dear," she said softly. "Don't you give Connie another thought."

Chelsea blinked back tears and gave a stiff nod. She took one last look over at the baby. Molly was staring out the window, bouncing on her toes to keep Connie quiet. Connie looked over at Chelsea. Her little head was bobbing up and down. She had that scrunched-up, old-man-with-indigestion look on her face that signaled she was about to squall.

"Tell Molly—" Chelsea began, then stopped herself.

"Tell her what, dear?"

Chelsea sighed. "Tell her Connie doesn't like to be bounced so hard. She . . . well, she likes rocking better."

"I'll tell her," Fiona said. "I promise."

Chelsea turned and followed her friends out into the hall.

"All right?" Kate asked when Fiona closed the door behind them.

"Yeah. At least, I know I'll get over it. Eventually."

Grace opened the envelope and whistled softly. "There's eight hundred dollars in here."

"Eight hundred bucks?" Chelsea asked. "I guess I'll get over it quicker than I thought." She shook her head regretfully. "You know, Molly didn't even bother to say thanks. She didn't even ask how Connie had been."

"Yeah, she's no prize as a human being," Grace agreed.

Chelsea looked at her sharply. "And that means she's probably not going to be much of a mother, either. Doesn't it?"

"I got the feeling Fiona will be Connie's mother more than Molly," Kate said. "She seemed nice, at least."

"Eight hundred dollars nice," Grace pointed out. "At least Connie will never go hungry. I imagine they'll have her signed up for one of those exclusive yuppie nursery schools in a few months. You know, where they teach kids to play the violin and do quantum physics at age two."

"Nothing I can do about it, anyway," Chelsea admitted. "And there's about a billion kids on the planet with more to worry about than Connie has."

"So should we save some of this money?" Kate wondered, taking the envelope from Grace. "Or should we spend it all?"

"Let's take a vote," Grace suggested. "All in favor of spending it all, run for the elevator!"

The three of them dashed down the hall.

"So this is what you do all evening, lie around watching the television?" Luis demanded. He was standing between the living room and the dining room that had been turned into Marta's bedroom.

Symbolic, Alec thought from his position on the couch. He looked past Luis to see Marta in her makeshift room, writing in a little book that looked like a diary. Maybe he was paranoid, but it seemed to Alec that Luis constantly managed to get between him and Marta.

"Pretty much," Alec admitted. "Some nights I go out."

"That's right," Luis said. "Some nights you go out and burn up people's homes."

"Daddy," Marta warned distractedly.

She was like United Nations peacekeeping troops, wearily trying to place herself between warring factions.

"Television rots your brain," Luis said. "You should read a book." He marched over and flicked off the set.

Alec felt his jaw grow tense. The remote control was in his hand. It would be easy to switch the set back on, but then, it would be as easy for Luis to switch it right back off. Somewhere in there Alec was going to get hurt, or worse yet, fired. Justin had been right weeks ago when he'd told Alec he was crazy, getting involved with his boss's daughter. It was a no-win situation. If Alec looked the other way and took whatever Luis handed him, Luis would think he was a weakling who wouldn't stand up for himself. Marta would probably think the same thing. On the other hand, defiance had its own risks.

He decided to compromise. Sarcasm was a compromise. "What's the last book you read, Luis?" That would fix him.

"I was reading that new book by Gabriel Garcia Marquez," Luis said promptly. "You know, for entertainment. Plus, I was finishing *Stilwell and the American Experience in China*. I don't know enough about the history of World War Two in China and Burma. I say *was* finishing," he added, "because it was burned up in the fire."

Alec stared at him. So much for sarcasm. So Luis got up every morning, ran ten miles, put in a full day of work, then spent the evening catching up on China and Burma. He probably did aerobics in his sleep while dreaming of new designs for computer chips.

"How did the apartment hunting go today?" Alec asked, as nicely as he could manage.

"I have some leads. Tomorrow the insurance adjustor is coming to look at the damage. I'm going to meet him during my lunch hour, so I'll need you to cover for me."

Great. That meant no lunch, Alec realized. And if Luis dragged him on another marathon in the morning, he'd be screaming with hunger by noon. "No problem," Alec said.

He wished Justin had hung around for the weekend. At least then he could go down to the boathouse. But no, Justin was off on his boat, and he'd even taken Mooch along. Kate and Chelsea and Grace were all away too, the traitors. No one was left to rescue him, to provide distraction. Unless you counted Connor.

"Excuse me," Alec said, climbing up from the couch. He took the stairs two at a time and knocked on Connor's door. "You home?"

"Come in," Connor called.

Alec opened the door. Connor was lying on his bed, reading a dusty book of poetry. "You too?" Alec asked. "Am I the only person who watches TV?"

"Things getting a little tense with the in-laws, are they?" Connor asked, grinning.

"Why don't you come down for a while?"

Connor laughed. "I've never heard you sound quite so desperate. Why would I go downstairs when I'm perfectly comfortable up here, where there are no psychotic Mexicans?"

"He's not Mexican," Alec said. "He's been in the country twenty years. He's a citizen."

"I notice you don't deny he's psychotic, though."

"No argument there. He won't let me watch TV. He says I should read a book."

"And so you should."

"I'll give you five bucks to come downstairs. I can't just go hide in my room. That would be admitting defeat."

"Five? That wouldn't buy me a six-pack."

"Ten."

Connor rolled off his bed. "Ten dollars, for one hour."

Alec sighed and fished the money out of his pocket. "You're scum, you know."

"For twenty I'll break your leg so you don't have to go running in the morning," Connor offered.

"No good," Alec said glumly. "I can get Luis to break any one of my bones for nothing."

THIRTEEN

Grace awoke the next morning to the sound of a ringing phone. She grabbed it on the third ring. "Good morning," said a chirpy voice. "This is your wake-up—"

"Yeah, yeah, whatever you say," Grace grunted. She replaced the receiver clumsily and fell back onto her pillow. Sleep drew her down again, but not for long.

Suddenly her eyes flew open. She was in New York.

She threw back her covers, went to the window, and opened the blinds, revealing the magnificent vista of a brick wall only a few yards away. Dusty indirect light filtered down, filling the room with gray gloom.

"Get up, we're in New York!" she announced happily to Kate and Chelsea, who had shared the other bed last night.

"Let's kill her," Kate groaned.

"What happened to you not being a morning person, Grace?" Chelsea demanded.

"Why should I jump out of bed when all I'm going to see is Ocean City?" Grace said. "Today I have New York. The Big Apple."

"Like I said before, the city that never sleeps." Kate yawned. "I used to think that sounded romantic. Now I realize it's because they do road construction at three in the morning, street sweeping at four, and ambulance races at five."

"Let's call room service for breakfast," Grace suggested. She fished in the desk drawer and found the room-service menu. "Bacon and eggs, thirteen ninety-five. Wow."

"You sound like Kate," Chelsea chided, stretching up on her toes, arms over her head. "We have Fiona's money. Put me down for a twenty-dollar breakfast."

"I want a muffin and some tea," Kate said. "Maybe a glass of juice."

"Good news," Grace said. "That only comes to twelve dollars."

Over breakfast, and in between drying their hair and applying makeup, the girls tried to agree, without much success, on how to spend the day.

"We shouldn't separate," Kate said. "I mean, this is the big city."

"Kate," Grace chided as she searched the room for a missing shoe, "I think it's time you got over the small-town girl thing. In a few weeks, you'll be living here full-time."

"I'll be on campus," Kate said with a shrug. "Besides, it's not me I'm worried about. It's the two of you—Miss Innocent and Miss Not-So-Innocent."

"I think I'll be safe enough at the Museum of Modern Art, *Mother*," Chelsea said, shooting Kate an annoyed look.

Grace laughed and popped the last piece of bacon into her mouth. "You've got to let the girl go sooner or later, Kate," she teased. "Chelsea's practically all grown up now."

"Fine, go ahead and laugh, but if either of you gets mugged, don't blame me."

"What would you do if we got mugged and you were there?" Grace asked. "Help us scream?"

Kate rolled back her sleeve and flexed her biceps. "I can take care of myself," she said with a grin.

"That's why Justin wants you on the boat with him," Grace said slyly. "Another strong arm to hoist the sails." Kate's face darkened and Grace instantly regretted her words. She didn't want to start the day exchanging barbs with Kate. Not when they'd been getting along so well lately.

"I might decide to give him my strong arm," Kate said defiantly. "I'm considering it."

"You're what?" Chelsea demanded. "You are kidding, aren't you?"

Kate shrugged and swallowed her herbal tea. "I told him I'd consider it. He's going to Europe, you know. It's some sort of race or something, so he says it would be relatively safe. Then he's going to cruise the Mediterranean."

Grace stared at Kate, stunned. *Europe?* Kate and Justin on his boat, sailing the Mediterranean? It wasn't that she was jealous of the two of them being together. That was ancient history, and now that she had David in her life, well . . . she hadn't given Justin a thought in quite a while.

But she would give anything to be offered an opportunity like that. Anything. And Kate was making it sound like it was only a possibility among many.

"When were you planning on deciding, Kate?" Chelsea asked, sounding increasingly irate. "I mean, we're supposed to room together."

"Excuse me? Is this the same girl who was twelve seconds away from getting married? I wasn't aware I had to consult with you on every decision I make," Kate said. "You certainly don't."

"Well," Grace said brightly, "I guess it's a good thing we're all going off in our own directions, after all."

"Look, if you sail away with Justin, it might change some decisions of my own," Chelsea muttered thoughtfully.

"I wouldn't worry about it too much," Kate said briskly as she ran a brush through her hair.

144

"You should make your own decisions anyway."

"Two minutes ago you didn't want me deciding to go to the museum by myself," Chelsea pointed out.

"I'm having enough trouble with this, all right?" Kate snapped. "One way I lose going to college. The other way I lose Justin. Either way I lose, so I don't need additional pressure." She stormed across the room. "I'm out of here. I'll see you guys later." At the door, she hesitated. "Back here by six?"

"Fine," Chelsea said.

Kate didn't wait for Grace's answer.

As soon as the door closed behind Kate, Grace turned to Chelsea. "You're her best friend. What's she going to do?"

Chelsea shook her head grimly. "Too close to call. But whichever way she goes, she'll decide soon. Kate can't stand indecision. She needs to have a clear goal in front of her or she goes crazy."

"Speaking of goals, I'm out of here," Grace said. "Ride down with me?"

Chelsea shook her head. She looked a little embarrassed. "I'm going to try to call Connor first."

Grace nodded. "What are you going to tell him?"

"That Connie's going to be fine," Chelsea said. "I guess you wouldn't expect him to care, would you?"

"Actually, I kind of guessed that he might

care," Grace said. "He's all right, deep down."

"Very deep down," Chelsea agreed with a laugh.

"It's funny," Grace said thoughtfully. "All three of us ended up with pretty great guys this summer. And Alec ended up with a really cool girl." She paused for a second to think. "I wonder how many of us will still be together a month from now."

"Quite a trip, huh?" the man beside Grace in the elevator said.

She checked to make sure he was talking to her. There were fifteen other people crammed into the overheated, stuffy little elevator. But yes, he was looking directly at her. Not bad-looking, but too old for this to be a flirtation. Probably. She nodded at him noncommittally. The elevator ride was taking an eternity.

"First time up here?"

"First time in New York," Grace admitted. *First time much of anywhere*, she thought.

"I come up here every month or so," the man said.

"Does the view change that much?"

"Same view each time, aside from weather changes," he answered, adding cryptically, "It's the perspective that changes."

The elevator slowed to a stop and the crowd piled out gratefully, rushing toward the doors and open air.

Grace had expected the view to be stunning, and she wasn't disappointed. Eighty-six floors up, the Empire State Building opened onto an observation platform that revealed the world in a way that Grace had never experienced. The earth far below was a three-dimensional puzzle drawn with a ruler, all straight lines up and straight lines across. Straight lines to define the boxy air conditioning and elevator machinery that was piled on tar-black roofs. Sheer walls like windowed cliffs that soared up from the choked streets, reaching not for the sky, it seemed to Grace, but merely for the chance to be noticed, cowering at the feet of the Empire State.

You could see, almost, as you worked your way around the platform, that Manhattan was an island. You could see the Hudson and the East rivers. You could see Central Park. It was easy to pick out the other tall buildings—the World Trade Center towers, the Chrysler Building.

But for Grace it wasn't a view made up of separate pieces. It was a single work of art, a maze of incredible complexity, constructed of concrete and brick and granite, in colors of buff and gray and dirty white. Not hundreds or thousands of buildings, but tens of thousands. Hundreds of thousands of cars on the streets, tiny, slow-crawling rectangles of color. And within the maze, millions of people, all somehow living their lives, doing their jobs, eating and drinking and taking out the trash.

She was invisible against this backdrop. She was insignificant. Everything she had done, everything she'd seen and known and guessed at could drop into this monumental creation and disappear without a ripple.

She looked out beyond the city, over the river where haze obliterated details. All this, this overpowering complexity, this sheer crushing mass, was only one city, in one state, in one country. One small slice of what the world had to offer.

She had spent eighteen years in one place. Walking one beach, when all the world's continents were bordered by beaches. She'd watched the sun set over one bay. And how many bays and how many sunsets in how many places had she not yet seen?

It was if she'd read only the first paragraph of a book. Heard the first notes of a symphony.

All her life Grace had felt a deep unhappiness with what she'd seen as her imprisonment in a tiny resort town called Ocean City. She'd yearned to escape, but she'd never had the courage to take even the first step. All she had known was that she wanted out.

And yet she hadn't gotten out. She hadn't gotten anywhere.

Grace smiled sadly. Of course she hadn't escaped. As powerfully as she had felt that need, it wasn't enough. Now, as she looked out from a thousand feet in the air over this one marvel in a universe of marvels, she understood. So much more compelling than the hatred of the old was the desire for the new. It wasn't about hating Ocean City, it couldn't be.

It had to be about this new emotion that had overcome her here, unexpectedly, in the air right below the clouds. The hunger for the new. The need to see and smell and touch and experience. This was the need that would drive out the need for drink and replace all her fear and doubt with hope.

She smiled. She laughed out loud. She held the railing with both hands and threw back her head, staring up at the giant needle that pointed straight to the sun.

"So what do you think?"

It was the man from the elevator, looking at her speculatively. Grace shook her head and searched for words. At last she shrugged. "I guess I'd sound like a complete tourist dweeb if I said that I've discovered the meaning of my life."

"Are you kidding?" he answered. "No surprise to me, honey. I'm a New Yorker. I mean, where else you going to find the meaning of life? Cleveland?"

According to Kate's guidebook, it was easy to take the subway from the hotel to Columbia. And much cheaper than a cab. Unfortunately—or fortunately, depending on your point of view—Kate had heard a few too many scary stories about

New York subways. Once she started school, she knew she'd probably have to ride the subways, but with a lot of Fiona's money in her pocket, it seemed like a better, wiser thing to take a cab.

The hotel doorman took ten minutes flagging one down. And the cab driver wasn't happy when she told him her destination.

"Columbia?" he cried in a thick foreign accent.

"It's a university," Kate explained. The driver's cab license, stuck on the plexiglas partition between the front and back seat, said Phong Nguyen. Vietnamese, Kate thought, or maybe Cambodian.

"I know wha' Columbia is, lady," he said. "I bee' drivin' here this city ni' year."

"Well, that's where I want to go. Is there a problem?"

"Proble' is no fare back."

"Excuse me?"

The driver uttered an unrecognizable curse and yanked the cab into traffic, accelerating at breakneck speed until he slammed on the brakes at a red light. "No fare coming back, understan'?"

"Oh. You're saying if you go up to Columbia you won't get another passenger coming back this way?"

"Tha's wha' I said. No fare back."

"I'm sorry, but how else am I going to get there?"

The driver shrugged. "Why you go the'?"

"I'm going to be a student in the fall." The light changed, and she was slammed back against the seat as the cab accelerated. Something was rattling as if it was ready to fall off. Kate hoped it wasn't anything major. Like a wheel.

"Ah," the driver said. "My son go NYU."

"New York University? Your son?"

"Tha's righ'. Two year now, two more to go. Wha' you study?"

Kate shrugged. Somehow it seemed strange and a little unreal, talking about what she was going to take in college. "I'm going to major in political science," she said.

"My son, matt."

"I'm sorry?"

"Matt. One, two, three." The driver held up his fingers and counted off.

"Oh, mathematics?" Kate said. "He must be smart."

"Ver' smar'," the driver said proudly. "He work hard. Make lo' money, then I don' drive cab." He laughed at this possibility and Kate joined in.

"Where are you from?" Kate asked.

"Vietnam. You study politics you lear' 'bout Vietnam." He laughed again.

"I guess I will," she said.

"But ten year here in New York America."

"You came from Vietnam ten years ago?"

The driver shook his head. "Before tha' one year in Thailand. Refugee camp. We go there by boat. Then," he made a shooing gesture with his free hand. "Thai people send us back to Vietnam. So we build new boat, one year. Whole village. Ver' bad. Fi' week in boat. Many people die, no water. This ti' we get to Hong Kong." He held up two fingers. "Two year in refugee camp there."

"Two years," Kate echoed.

"I learn English the'." He grinned at her in the rearview mirror. "Pretty good, huh?"

"Pretty good," she agreed. "I guess you must have wanted to get here awfully badly."

The driver nodded. "My wi' she stay in camp Hong Kong. Too sick to go here, you unnerstan'?"

"You had to leave your wife there?" Kate could not keep the horror out of her voice.

"She die long time. She say go for our son." The driver nodded and was silent for a while. Then he brightened. "Now thi' my country. No more Vietnam. My son go to college just like you. My wi' be ver' happy if she see. I be' my son he smart as you," he added, looking challengingly into the mirror.

Kate smiled. There was no mistaking the pride in the man's voice. "If he's a math major," she conceded, "he's probably smarter."

The driver let her out on 116th Street. She paid him and added a ridiculously large tip. Well,

152

what the hell, Kate decided. It was Fiona's money, anyway.

She was near Butler Library, an imposing classical building with huge columns, and the names of the great Greeks—Homer, Sophocles, Plato, and the rest of the usual suspects—chiseled in letters that looked three feet high.

She walked around to the front of the building. The campus had a somewhat deserted feel to it, here in the middle of summer with the start of the fall semester still weeks away. Across a broad lawn on the other side of College Walk stood the statue of Alma Mater, a rather grim-looking woman with an open book on her knees.

Kate had seen all of it before, of course, with Chelsea and her father. Columbia was his alma mater, and he'd shown them everything with a definite enthusiasm and affection that had amused Kate at the time. Mr. Lennox was normally a little on the stiff side.

She hadn't expected to see the campus again until orientation, but she was glad to have the chance to look at it all again. This time she wasn't merely a soon-to-be high school graduate with big dreams. She was a person who, it seemed to her, had aged many years in the few weeks of summer. She wanted to give the campus a fair chance in its competition against Justin for possession of her heart.

She walked up the steps to the library and

went inside. Rows of computer catalog terminals sat almost unused, awaiting the new influx of students. Millions of books were housed in the library in cramped, stuffy stacks. The place smelled of dust, and faintly of mildew. It seemed to radiate some of the tension and exhaustion of all the countless thousands who had crammed frantically here in the last hours before a final exam. But it seemed to echo as well the hopes of people who had sacrificed greatly for the chance to learn.

It was definitely *not* the ocean. It was not the south of France, or the north of Italy, or the islands of Greece. And it wasn't any more inviting, or any less intimidating, than it had been when she had seen it last.

And yet, Kate saw something new this time, something she hadn't quite noticed when she'd arrived by limousine. Somehow the campus, the buildings, the books in this library, the simple *idea* of the place, seemed so much more important when you arrived by cab.

FOURTEEN

Justin spread out the chart and held it down by placing a can of soda on one corner and his foot on the other. He leaned on the tiller with his left arm and tried to read the chart, but the breeze was making things difficult. He could take it below, but these were busy waters and he tried to minimize the time spent below in the shelter of the cabin. It would be awfully easy for some tanker captain to overlook him. And his little boat was not going to come out the winner in a collision with a supertanker.

He traced his route and compared the position he'd calculated the hard way with the position he'd been given electronically with the touch of a button. They were within a second of latitude, and right on the longitude.

"Right on the money, Mooch," he announced. Mooch, who was dozing near Justin's feet, gave a lone wag of his tail.

After the first day out, Justin had stopped worrying about the way he talked to himself—and to Mooch. When Kate came with him, he'd have someone to actually converse with. And someone to stand watch while he got some real sleep. It would take a couple of weeks before Kate would feel confident, probably, but as smart as she was, he knew she'd learn the basics in no time.

He yawned. He hadn't really slept the night before, just dozed on deck with one eye open while the boat made way under autopilot.

The sun was still high in the sky and the heat made him feel a little woozy. Even the occasional shower of cold spray failed to revive him completely. The shoreline of Fire Island was too far off and too shrouded in haze for him to make out details, but he was certain of where he was—73 degrees, 1 minute west longitude, 40 degrees, 32 minutes, and 10 seconds north latitude.

He'd gone far enough in this direction. It was time to turn about and begin the more demanding task of sailing south again, in the teeth of the prevailing wind. There was only one thing he needed to consider. The weather service was tracking a minor storm rolling up the east coast with expected winds of twenty-five knots. Twenty-five-knot winds were considered a strong breeze, right at the line between heading for shelter and toughing it out.

He looked down at the chart. There was

plenty of shelter he could reach before the storm arrived. But he could expect to run into much worse weather someday when he was too far to reach a safe port. And you never really knew how your equipment would perform until it was under stress.

"I'm tired, though," he told Mooch, imagining a safe anchorage and six or eight hours of sleep. Mooch yawned and rolled onto his back, legs pointed skyward like a four-poster bed.

"All the more reason," Justin argued back. "I should see what I can do under pressure. See if I'm really up for big-time sailing. I can't be talking about crossing the Atlantic if I can't ride out a minor blow."

Of course, if he ended up losing his boat, that wouldn't be too good either.

"Take a southerly heading, keep an ear on the weather service, and if it gets any worse than they've said so far, bail and run for shelter," he said, announcing his decision to a sea gull that was hanging in the air a few feet from his mainsail. "You coming?" he asked the gull. Mooch opened one eye and sniffed the air, suddenly alert to the possibility of an afternoon snack. He snarled and the gull swooped away.

Justin brought the boat around and set her on a port tack, bearing away from the coast. He couldn't head in a straight line back to Ocean City, since that would mean the impossibility of sailing directly into the wind. Instead he would be traveling at an angle to the wind and tacking—moving in zigzags across the water. As a result, the trip back would cover many more miles than the trip up.

"See, Mooch," he said, "here's how we should be doing this. Kate should be down below, making lunch and fixing you up a big bowl of dog slop. We'd eat, and then I'd go below for a rest and let her take over. After a few hours' sleep I'd come back up, bring her a fresh cup of coffee, and we'd watch the sun go down together."

That wasn't such a bad vision, was it? Kate and him together, free, independent, and madly in love. "Maybe we'd make port that night, drop anchor in a peaceful little harbor, take the dinghy ashore to some quaint Italian fishing village and have dinner in an outdoor cafe. We'd drink red wine and have conversations with the locals in sign language and pidgin English. And later, we'd row back out to the boat and make love all night."

Mooch shifted position on the sunny deck and let out a low groan. "What?" Justin asked. "Is there something wrong with that idea? Am I missing something, or is that pretty close to paradise?"

He nodded contentedly. How could Kate not see? How could she possibly decide against coming? "She can't," he said. "No way."

If only she had come along on this trip rather than going to New York. She'd have seen it all firsthand. You could not breathe this pure salt air and not want to breathe it every day of your life. You could not feel the wind, ride the wind, know that the wind could take you anywhere, and not want that same feeling every day of your life. You could not experience the utter independence, the complete isolation from all the world's complications, and not crave that same freedom every day.

You couldn't. She couldn't.

"Hi, Alec, it's me, Chelsea. Is Connor there?"

"He's somewhere around, I think. CONNOR! PHONE! He's coming. He's upstairs."

"Okay. So, how's everything around the old homestead?"

"Swell."

"You don't sound very sincere."

"Don't I?"

"No. Is Luis nearby or something?"

"Yes, yes, as a matter of fact. That's exactly right."

"Bummer. Is he driving you nuts?"

"That would certainly be one way of putting it."

"Let's see. On a scale of one to ten, one being a perfect world with universal love and peace, and ten being a nightmare existence, a living hell, where would you be?"

"Eleven. But, gee, let's not talk about little old me, how's the big city?"

"Very big."

"Here's Connor."

"Chelsea?"

"Hi, sweetheart."

"Hi, Chelsea."

"I said, hi *sweetheart*."

"Uh-huh."

"Baby. Wonder lips. My one true love."

"Uh-huh. You do realize I'm not alone?"

"Sure. I still want you to call me sugar, you know, like you do, and tell me how much you love me and want me and can't sleep at night because you're thinking about me."

"Mmm, I don't think so. Did I mention Alec and Luis are both right here?"

"I know. But you should call me sweet cheeks and say you love me. You did when I called you yesterday evening."

"Let me guess—you're not alone, either, and Grace and Kate are both hanging on your every word and laughing hysterically as you torture me."

"You're so smart. That's why I love you. Actually, I really did miss you. I went to the Museum of Modern Art today, and the Guggenheim. Amazing, amazing, amazing."

"So, amazing, were they?"

"One of these days it will be the special exhibition of works by Chelsea Lennox hanging at MOMA. Or the Guggenheim."

"I believe it."

"I really do love you."

"Me too."

"I guess that's as much as I'm going to get out of you," Chelsea said. "This isn't nearly as much fun as it would be if you were here. You'd enjoy it. You know how you love to look at all the different types of people on the boardwalk? New York is that times ten."

"I'll have to get up there someday."

"Yeah. Well, I'll be going to school here and all."

"That will make it convenient for me."

"Damn."

"What?"

"It makes me mad," Chelsea said. "It is definitely *not* metaphysically correct. You should be here. You should have come with me today."

"You had Kate and Grace."

"No, they did other stuff. Besides, they're fun, but they're not the same kind of fun."

"I should hope not."

"We're going out to get Chinese food now. Spending some more of Fiona's money. Which reminds me, did I make it clear enough that I think she's going to be okay for Connie? I didn't want you to worry."

"You told me," Connor assured her. "I'm not worried. Not much I can do, anyway, is there? And it does sound like it will all work out all right."

"Damn."

"Yes. I agree."

"I wish you were here, Connor. I need you to kiss me."

"Oh, all right, I miss you, too."

"Are you being careful?" Chelsea asked. "What if you get picked up or something? I don't think you should go to work. I don't think you should leave the house. What if Immigration gets you and I'm up here?"

"Don't worry, sweetheart. Watch your damn TV, Alec, and no clever remarks."

"That's telling him. Well, Kate's hungry. We better get going."

"Okay. Coming home day after tomorrow, huh?"

"That's the plan. We figured since we have money and all, why not take the extra day? Tomorrow we're all playing tourist together. We're going to the Statue of Liberty and we're going to try and get in to see a TV show being taped. Joan Rivers or something. Have I mentioned I love you?"

"I love you."

"And I miss you."

"I miss you too."

"Sweetheart."

"Baby. Shut up, Alec."

"Bye-bye."

"Bye."

"Wait. I love you."

FIFTEEN

Through the open dining-room window the next day, Marta could hear Alec's footsteps coming up the stairs. She heard him sigh before opening the door. It amazed her that he came home at all. Work had to be a breeze compared to having her father in his face here at the house.

She wheeled into the front hall, hoping to catch him before her father did. But Luis was already waiting, hands on hips, nodding his head at Alec. Alec hesitated for a moment, then squared his shoulders and entered the house.

"Afternoon, Luis. Hi, Marta."

"Daniels," Luis said. "Sad, terrible news."

Alec sighed. "Oh?" he asked neutrally.

"I found a place."

Marta smothered a smile as the light began to dawn in Alec's eyes. "You did?"

Luis nodded. "Guy got arrested for selling cocaine. Great apartment, ocean view, the whole thing. The landlord cut the rent two hundred so I can afford it. That way he can be sure he doesn't get another scuzzball tenant."

"So it's available . . . when?"

Luis clapped a hand on Alec's shoulder. "It's available now. We'd be gone already, only I knew you'd want to say good-bye to me in person."

Amazingly, Alec didn't smile. When he looked over at Marta, she thought she saw a hint of sadness in his eyes. Maybe even more than a hint.

"Come on, Marta, let's get out of here before Daniels burns up this place too."

"I'm not quite ready to leave yet, Daddy," Marta said. She'd been planning this. Her father had wanted to delay his grand exit until Alec got home, and Marta had waited for this moment, too.

"Get your things, honey," Luis said. "What few things you have left that weren't burned up."

"I think we need to have a little talk first," Marta said. She nodded toward the living room. Alec and her father stared at each other indecisively for a moment, then followed her as she began to wheel away.

When they got there, Alec sat stiffly on the La-Z-Boy, leaning forward with his elbows on his knees. Luis stood in front of the couch, arms crossed over his chest.

"Boys," Marta began. "I would say *men*, but given the way you two have been acting, I don't think that would be completely accurate."

Her father cocked an eyebrow at her, but she ignored him. "Point number one. I want to clear something up, not that I haven't tried to explain this already." She glared at her father. "*I'm* the one who lit the candle. *I'm* the one who should have remembered it was lit. So *I'm* the one who's responsible for burning down the apartment."

"Wait a minute," Alec protested. "I was there too. I should have realized it was dangerous."

"Which brings us to point number two, Alec," Marta continued. "I thought we'd been through all this before, but you don't seem to have gotten the message. See, I'm your girlfriend, not your wife, not your daughter, not your little sister. I don't need you taking the blame for me."

"It's not that, it's . . . well, I mean, let's be honest. I was the guy carrying you." Marta saw her father's eyes grow dark and malevolent. She was pretty sure Alec noticed, too, but he kept on going anyway. "I had full movement within the apartment. It would have been much easier for me to go and check the living room than it was for you."

Marta held up her hand. "Would you listen to me, Alec? You're not doing me any favors by trying to take responsibility for everything. See, if you take the blame when things go wrong, then you can take the credit when things go right. It was my home, I was the host, it was my turf, it was my job to remember the damn candle, all right?" She calmed herself down and took a few breaths. "The whole world is ready to pat me on the head and say, 'Hey, you're doing real well *for a crip*.' I don't want to be a good student *for a crip*, or funny *for a crip*, or pretty *for a crip*. I don't need extra points, all right?"

Alec met her eyes, and for the first time Marta thought she saw understanding begin to dawn there. It wasn't really his fault, of course. He was physically perfect as well as smart. How could he *not* be tempted to see her in a condescending light?

She pointed her finger at him. "I love you, Alec, but you coddle me, you pity me, you treat me like your little sister ever again, and it's over." She softened when she saw the look of panic on his face. "Of course," she added with a slight smile, "I can sometimes still use a little help getting around."

"Wait one minute here," her father interrupted. "You won't be needing his help. See, I've been around this boy enough lately to be disappointed. I know this sounds like I'm old-fashioned, but I'm old-fashioned." He stared down at Alec. "I'll tell you this to your face," he said. "I'm not too impressed, all right? You're an okay lifeguard, but as a man for my daughter, I don't think so."

"Which brings me to point number three," Marta said. "I'm eighteen, Daddy."

"I'm thirty-nine," Luis countered. "And I'm

your father. I know a little bit more about people than you do."

"Daddy, do you realize that in less than a month I'll be going away to college?"

Her father's expression was stony.

"I'll be on my own, in a dorm five hundred miles from you. I won't have you to tell me whom I should or shouldn't be with."

"As long as you aren't with this one." He pointed contemptuously at Alec.

"I'll be with whomever I want, Daddy. And I'll be with them as much as I want, too. I'm not a little girl anymore. I make my own decisions."

"If this is what you want, then I don't think much of your decisions," her father sneered. But even as he spoke, he somehow seemed a little deflated.

It hasn't really sunk in yet, Marta realized. *He doesn't realize how soon I'll be going.* "Actually, Daddy," she said gently, "I think you're full of it. I think you wouldn't approve of any man who . . . who looked like he was taking me away."

"Oh, so now he's taking you away," her father said. "If that's what you call it."

"I know you two are different in some ways," Marta said. Her father snorted and Alec rolled his eyes. "But you are the same in one big, important way."

"Don't think that because we're both on the Beach Patrol—" Luis began.

"No. I meant that you are both men with some . . . I don't know, maybe it's integrity. I think that's it." Marta smiled at their uncertain reactions. "I could suspect either of you, or both of you, of being stupid, of being stubborn, of being annoying. Adolescent. Immature. Sometimes ridiculous. But I could never suspect either of you of being low or mean or cruel."

"Please, don't compare me to this boy," her father said angrily.

"Look," Marta snapped, finally losing patience, "I'm not a piece of property. I'm sick of you two acting like you're fighting for control of me. I'm in control of me."

"I'm still your father," Luis answered.

"And I'm *your* daughter," Marta agreed. "And you ought to know better than to expect any daughter of yours to be some weak-willed little wallflower who does whatever she's told. Did you raise me to be strong and independent, or did you raise me to be your *little* girl?"

Her father started to answer back, but reconsidered. After a moment, he tried again, but the retort died before reaching his lips. Suddenly he smacked his right fist into the palm of his left hand and muttered a long string of curses in Spanish.

Marta relaxed and allowed herself a grin. "Can't think of an answer, can you?"

"I'm working on one!" her father said. "Give me a minute."

"Here's my decision," Marta said. "Alec has asked me to live here with him until the end of summer. I've decided not to do that. It's too soon." Her father relaxed visibly. Alec gave her a resigned smile. "Anyway, at college I'll see what life is like on my own. Alec, you'll be close by. I hope you'll still come to see me."

"You know I will."

Her father muttered darkly, but without much conviction.

"Good, good." Marta looked at Alec, who was smiling back at her in amusement. She looked at her father, who seemed embarrassed and frustrated. For a moment she thought about asking the two of them to shake hands, but that, she decided, might be pushing her luck too far.

"Now, let's go check out the new place, Daddy," she said, wheeling toward the door.

"Stay away from matches, Daniels," her father growled over his shoulder.

Alec had the next day off. No Luis at work. No Luis at home. No Luis that evening, either. Alec and Marta were going out to a movie, and she'd agreed to meet him here at the house so he could avoid running into her father. All in all, a perfect Luis-free day.

In the meantime, the Cincinnati Reds were playing the Atlanta Braves on the cable sports channel. He had complete command of the La-Z-Boy and unchallenged control of the remote. He had a six-pack of Pepsi, a bag of nacho-cheese-flavored Doritos, and a can of bean dip. He had done enough running with Luis to work off ten bags of Doritos.

He punched the remote and the game came on. Perfect. Right in time for the first pitch. As the batter swung, he heard Connor clumping up the porch steps in his heavy work boots.

"Hi, honey, I'm home," Connor said, tossing his hard hat in the general direction of the couch.

"How was your day at the office, dear?" Alec asked.

"Hot, dirty, and generally unpleasant," Connor said. "Bloody storm yesterday, a bloody sauna today." He flopped down on the couch. "Corn chips?" he asked sardonically. "Do you really think you should let yourself go like that? There's some granola bars in the kitchen."

"Ha," Alec said. "Do you really think that after Luis you can get a rise out of me? Amateur."

Connor gazed at the TV indifferently. "Baseball. All the relaxation of watching grass grow, with none of the excitement."

"Communist."

"So, enjoying your newfound freedom?"

Alec grinned. "I slept like a baby last night in the comfortable certainty that Luis would not be the first person I saw when I got up in the morning. I didn't even run at all today. And I slept until almost nine."

"You're a wild man," Connor commented.

The Cincinnati batter knocked a grounder straight toward the third baseman. But he was fast and racing toward first. "Out?" Alec cried. "No way! He was safe by a foot."

"He was out by two feet," Connor said. "Not that I care."

"I know he's out," Alec said, "but you have to support your team."

"Everything good now between you and Marta?"

Alec shot Connor a glance. "Everything was always fine between us."

"Uh-huh. You know, parents and in-laws are a big problem between lots of couples," he said wisely. "You should have dealt a little more firmly with that fellow."

"*You* deal firmly with him."

"I would have," Connor said, smirking. "At least I wouldn't have been reduced to paying someone to hang out with me."

Alec shrugged. "I'm alive. That's all I ever hoped for."

Connor said something under his breath. Alec gave him a dirty look. "Did you just call me a wimp?"

"Me?" Connor pretended to look surprised. "Of course not. I'd never say that." He executed a perfect dramatic pause. "Might think it. I'd never say it, though." He got up and started toward the stairs. "Best go shower away the day's dirt. Even though Chelsea's out of town, it doesn't mean I should let myself go."

Alec snorted. "Too late. You've let yourself go so long you're gone."

From the direction of the street Alec noticed the sound of doors slamming. He exchanged a glance with Connor.

"Think it's the girls getting back early?" Alec wondered. He hoped they wouldn't have to tell all their adventures until the game was over.

Connor slumped toward the window and pulled back the blind. "Not the girls," he said, sounding disappointed. "Could be movie stars. Could be the mafia."

"Mafia?"

"Yeah. Two rather large black limousines are parked out front."

Suddenly Connor turned around and stared wide-eyed at Alec. "Oh, no," he muttered. "I should never have given you a hard time over Luis. I have a very bad feeling about this."

SIXTEEN

"You know, it's kind of interesting, really," Chelsea remarked. "I mean, you're used to being on a highway and everyone's moving so quickly you never really get the chance to see what the individual white lines look like. Or notice those little reflector things."

Grace was sitting in the driver's seat of Kate's car, one hand lazily draped over the wheel, the other fiddling with the radio dial. "Yeah, and you don't get the chance to play peek-a-boo with the kid in the next car for a solid hour either."

"Do you guys see anything yet?" Kate called out. She was lying in the backseat, her bare feet stuck out over the side. She kept saying she was taking a nap, but she never seemed to fall asleep.

Chelsea looked up at the sky, partly cloudy now that yesterday's storm had passed. The sun was setting behind what looked like some fantastic, evil castle built of steel towers, silos, and huge conveyer belts. It was surrounded by wasteland and desolation. Probably some kind of cement factory or something, Chelsea decided. New Jersey, at least the part on either side of the highway, seemed to have a lot of factories.

"I can't see anything," Grace said. "And all I can get on the radio is evangelists, weather reports, and gardening tips—none of which seem to know anything about this mother of all traffic jams."

"I wanted to get home before nightfall," Kate said.

"Try walking," Grace said. "It would be faster."

"You know what I'm thinking about?" Chelsea asked.

"Does it involve the artistic possibilities of dividing lines?" Grace asked sarcastically.

"No. I was just remembering when Kate and I first drove into Ocean City," Chelsea said, calling the image up in her mind. "Actually, it wasn't Kate's first trip to O.C., but it was mine. I had to pee really bad. We met Alec briefly. He was driving in too, when we all had to stop for the toll bridge to go up." Chelsea thought back to the clean, salt air, the jet skiers on the bay, the tall condos silhouetted against the ocean. She looked around at the six lanes of nearly immobile cars. "I'd have to say that was a better drive."

"Ah, we were young then," Kate joked. "We were carefree and innocent."

"I'm still innocent," Chelsea said, unable to resist.

"That's *not* what I'm talking about," Kate said. "Or maybe it is. Who knew what was going to happen us back then? I thought I'd spend all my time working at Safe Seas, living in a cramped little apartment with Chelsea."

"That's only what you *told* yourself, Kate," Grace argued. "You went back to O.C. to find Justin again."

"Well, maybe. Unconsciously."

"I didn't go there looking to find Connor," Chelsea said.

"Nobody *looks* for Connor," Kate said. "He's like a stray cat. He shows up on your porch one day and then you're stuck with him."

Grace laughed in agreement. Chelsea poked her in retaliation, since Kate was too far away to reach. "You're speaking of the man I almost married," Chelsea said. Then she shrugged. "And may still."

She heard Kate sit up in the backseat. "You're not thinking about that again, are you?" Kate asked.

"I never really stopped thinking about," Chelsea admitted. "Why should I? Nothing's changed."

"I don't know, I figured after the whole thing with Molly and the baby and all . . . You know, I never did think it was a smart thing to do. People shouldn't get married at our age."

"You're not going to put us through that

whole wedding routine again, are you?" Grace asked Chelsea. "I mean, once for a laugh, sure."

"It's not like I've decided," Chelsea said defensively. "It's just that, you know, I missed him."

"I missed David, too," Grace said. "But we're not talking marriage. Honeymoon, sure. But not marriage."

"Unlike you and Kate, I have certain beliefs," Chelsea said. "Like the fact that it's supposed to be marriage first, *then* honeymoon. I know it's quaint, but I can't set aside what my church teaches because it gets in the way of me having a good time." She was sounding more pedantic than she'd meant to, but Kate and Grace were getting on her nerves. She sighed. "And anyway, that's not the reason we wanted to get married."

"There *was* that little matter of deportation," Grace noted.

"It wasn't that, either," Chelsea said. "I mean, sure, that was the reason it all started, but . . ." Her voice trailed off.

"I'm sure you missed Justin, too, didn't you, Kate?" Grace suggested. She shot Chelsea a conspiratorial look.

"Yes," Kate said flatly.

"On the other hand, you really enjoyed visiting Columbia," Grace said.

Kate emitted a loud sigh and lay back on the seat.

"Of course, you really can't compare being entombed for four years in some university library with sailing around the Mediterranean with a very good-looking and, as I remember him, very passionate guy."

"Grace, when I decide what I'm going to do," Kate replied irritably, "you'll be the last to know."

After that, everyone fell silent for a while. Traffic moved forward a few hundred yards, then stopped again. No doubt there was an eighteen-wheeler jackknifed up ahead somewhere, Chelsea decided. It could be midnight by the time they got home. Connor would probably be asleep. Tough. She'd wake him up. They would talk about everything that had happened to each of them while they were apart. Then there would be lots of kissing. She closed her eyes and imagined that part. Yes, she had definitely missed kissing him.

"I think I'm mature enough," Chelsea said.

"For what?" Kate asked.

Chelsea shrugged. Actually, she hadn't meant to speak out loud. "To make my own decisions," she said evasively.

"I'm not mature enough to make *that* decision," Grace said.

"Sure, Grace," Kate said laconically, "but you're not as mature as Chelsea. After all, sometimes Chelsea decides to clean up her room all by herself. About once a year. How's that for mature?"

"Very funny," Chelsea said.

"Sometimes she can actually remember to deposit her paycheck *before* she starts spending the money."

"And of course *you* are the soul of responsibility?" Chelsea demanded.

"Who balances your checkbook for you? Who goes through your shelf in the refrigerator and throws out your moldy yogurt before you eat it and die? Who has to make sure the letters you *think* you've mailed actually get mailed?"

Chelsea grinned sheepishly. Details had never been her strong suit. Maybe that much was true. But something Kate had said stuck in her mind. "Mail?" Chelsea asked. "What mail?"

"Before we left, to give one example. I found a letter on the table downstairs and mailed it for you."

"What letter?" Chelsea asked.

"To your parents."

"That's the letter I found stuck to the bottom of Connie's baby carrier," Grace said, laughing.

Chelsea sat bolt upright and clutched at the dashboard. "NO!"

"What's the matter?" Kate asked.

"We have to get out of this traffic," Chelsea cried. "It may be a matter of life and death."

"I am Albert Lennox, Chelsea's father. This is Michelle Rowe-Lennox, Chelsea's mother. Midshipman B.D. Lennox, Chelsea's older brother. And Mr.

178

Wilmer Cravath. Our lawyer. I gather from your accent that you must be Connor Riordan."

Connor stuck out his hand, which was ignored. He glanced over his shoulder to see Alec, grinning and slowly shaking his head.

"Um, come on in, please, won't you?" Connor said.

The four of them trooped in. Mr. Lennox, a balding man with gray temples, was wearing a conservatively cut dark gray pinstripe suit. He looked like what he was, an economics professor. Behind him came his very chic, very attractive wife, dressed in a tailored sky-blue suit. B.D. was approximately ten feet tall and wearing a blue uniform and shoes shined to a mirror finish. He removed his hat and held it under his arm. The lawyer was white and middle-aged, and glanced around with distaste at the shabby living room.

Connor held the door open as they passed, a slow, mournful, potentially volatile parade.

"I'll leave you all alone," Alec whispered in Connor's ear.

"Don't you abandon me, you coward."

"But you know how to handle in-laws," Alec said with a smirk.

"Ten bucks," Connor said.

"There's four of them," Alec countered. "There was only one Luis. We're talking at least twenty."

"Done. Whatever you do, though, don't leave me here alone with them. I may need a witness."

179

The group hovered by the couches, waiting until Connor joined them. Mr. Lennox seemed to be the spokesman. "Is Chelsea here?"

"Actually, uh, Mr. Lennox, sir, she's in New York. Should be back any minute, though."

"New York?" Mrs. Lennox snapped. "Why is she in New York?"

Why is Chelsea in New York? Well, Connor, he told himself, this ought to be an interesting explanation. "She went with Grace and Kate. They had to return something."

"Return what?" Mr. Lennox asked in his soft, slow voice.

Connor took a deep breath. "Would you all like to sit down? Would you like something to drink? Tea? Coffee?"

"Don't you want to break out some of your beer?" Alec asked gleefully.

Connor shot him a murderous look.

"I'll go make some tea," Alec volunteered. When he got to the kitchen, Connor noticed he left the door propped open.

Connor waved vaguely at the couches, and his four visitors sat down, mother and father on one couch, brother and lawyer on the other. Connor was left with the La-Z-Boy. He settled into it and tried not to twitch as he glanced around at their faces. Mrs. Lennox was beautiful, and could easily have passed for Chelsea's older sister. And B.D. looked a bit like his sister, if you could imagine Chelsea stretched way out and given the sort of cool appraising eyes that looked as if they were measuring you for a casket.

"You haven't explained why Chelsea is in New York," Mr. Lennox pressed.

He could lie. He could come up with some plausible story. He was very good at that. But sooner or later they'd get the truth out of Chelsea. Damn her! Where was she now that he needed her? And where was Alec?

He forced a smile. "The truth is, Chelsea's in New York returning a baby. The baby was left here by a young woman of my acquaintance who claimed at first that I was the father. Now she's changed her story, and Chelsea volunteered, along with Kate and Grace, to return the baby to her mother, who is now in New York."

There. The simple truth. It was an unusual tactic for him, but when you had no other choice . . .

"I see," Mr. Lennox said.

"I don't," Mrs. Lennox snapped. "We got a letter from Chelsea dated almost two weeks ago but postmarked only a few days back."

"Did you?" Connor asked brightly.

"In this letter she says that she has gotten married." Mrs. Lennox nearly choked on the word. "Married to you."

Connor's smile froze on his face.

"Oh, good, I didn't miss the fun part," Alec said, returning with a tray full of teacups and a pot. "All we have is honey," he added. "The sugar has ants in it."

The lawyer spoke for the first time. "The substance of the letter was that she had agreed to this union as part of a plan to allow you to claim U.S. residency. I gather you are in the country illegally."

Oh. So they knew that part, too. Connor felt all the tension, all the excitement, every emotion drain out of him. They had come with a lawyer. That could only mean that they'd intended to undo the marriage somehow. It was probably rather easy to do, really, when you could show that it had taken place under false pretenses.

Connor looked over at Alec, who was gazing at the ground and shaking his head. Nothing could be more depressing than seeing Alec actually feeling sorry for him.

"The wedding did not take place," Connor said in a low voice.

"Are you telling us the truth?" Mrs. Lennox rapped out the question.

"Mom," B.D. interjected. He had his father's quiet, restrained voice. "I don't think we need to start accusing anyone of lying."

Connor attempted a smile that died quickly. "I'd be offended, only the fact is, I've done my share of lying. Most recently, when I arrived at J.F.K. airport and the customs man asked how long I intended to stay here."

182

"So that was indeed your plan," Mr. Lennox asked. "To marry my daughter in order to obtain resident status."

"Yeah, that was it. In fact, it was something I'd thought about in general terms long before I met your daughter. I thought, well, maybe I'll meet some nice girl, get her to marry me, stay with her till I get my green card, then I'm on my way, free and legal."

The entire group stared at him in accusing silence.

"As it turned out, we didn't go ahead with the plan. I'll let Chelsea tell you how close we came. Let's just say it was measured in seconds."

"Lord," Mrs. Lennox said, putting a hand to her forehead.

"And I take it that the marriage is off now?" Mr. Lennox asked. "Permanently?"

Connor stared out the window and nodded almost imperceptibly. "It looks that way, doesn't it?"

SEVENTEEN

"Does your dad own a limo, by any chance?" Grace asked as they approached the house.

"No, but I'm sure it's him," Chelsea said anxiously. "He doesn't like renting cars in unfamiliar towns. He says that way you have to drive with a map in one hand the whole time. Oh, man, this is going to be really terrible."

The trip home had taken forever. It was nearly ten thirty, and they should have been back in Ocean City by six at the latest. They'd hit traffic jams all the way home, and to make matters worse, the car had overheated. They'd had to let it cool for an hour and hike to a gas station for water. It had been a nightmare trip, made infinitely worse by the realization that Kate had sent the stupid letter Chelsea had written—the one she had never intended to send.

"Is your dad a shouter?" Grace asked.

"No," Kate answered for her. "He's more a head shaker. You know—'Chelsea, I'm extremely disappointed in you.'"

"Yeah," Chelsea agreed. "My mom's the shouter."

Kate parked the car and Grace climbed out over the side. She stretched wearily. "Great trip, except for the last few hours. Changed my life."

Chelsea got out slowly. Her feet seemed to have turned to lead. She stared at the limo as a feeling of doom descended. The worst had happened. Her parents had gotten the letter. And they had showed up here, in Ocean City. They were in her house right now, probably making Connor wish he'd never met her. It was even possible, she realized, that they might try to have Connor deported. They might have decided that was the only way to keep her from marrying him.

Kate came up alongside her and put her arm around Chelsea's shoulder. "It's not an execution, Chels. We'll find a way to make it all work out."

Good old Kate. But she was wrong. In a way, this *was* an execution.

Chelsea paused at the door with her hand on the knob. *Don't cry, whatever you do. Don't cry*, she told herself.

She opened the door, with Kate and Grace close behind her.

The first thing she saw was B.D. standing in

a crouch, a fixed expression on his face and a baseball bat in his hands.

"B.D.!" she cried. She lunged toward him, horrified.

"Hey, Chels," B.D. said, breaking out in a welcoming smile. "About time you got back. We were starting to worry."

Chelsea noticed her father, tie loosened, sitting in the La-Z-Boy, holding one of Connor's Irish beers. Her mother was seated on the couch, with her shoes off, in animated conversation with Marta. Marta was making some point with her usual force. Alec was on the other couch, sipping a soda and staring at the TV. And, most surprising of all, Connor, apparently alive and well, was beside Alec, looking up at B.D. and laughing.

"What . . . what's going on?" Chelsea asked.

B.D. lowered the bat a little sheepishly. He came over and gave her a hug. "Sorry, I was trying to explain to your dumb foreigner boyfriend why baseball is the greatest game on earth." He released her and gave Grace a once-over before giving Kate a warm embrace.

"Hi, honey," her mother called out. "Was the traffic bad?"

Was the traffic bad? Was that what they'd come all the way to Ocean City to find out?

This scene was totally unreal. It was as if she were back at her parents' house and had just returned from a trip to the mall.

186

She shot a look at Connor. He shrugged. Apparently he was as bewildered as she was.

Kate, of course, knew the family well and went around hugging and saying hello and introducing Grace.

"I know you said you had a brother," Grace told Chelsea. "But I didn't know he was a big brother. Such a big brother."

"It's a double header," Alec offered, by way of contribution. He gestured toward the TV. "Cincinnati at Atlanta. Braves took the first game, and now we're top of the eighth, three to two."

My life's in total chaos. Does he really think I care? Chelsea wondered.

"I suppose you're wondering why we're here?" her father said.

"Kind of."

"We received a very strange letter."

"I know. I . . . It wasn't really supposed to get mailed." She hooked a thumb toward Kate and Grace. "My two brilliant roommates managed between them to mail it anyway."

"Yes, we deduced that something of the sort may have happened." He looked a little uncomfortable. "I told your mother it was silly, but—"

"Told *me* it was silly?" her mother protested. "Who was it who insisted we bring our lawyer?"

"You brought a *lawyer*?" Chelsea cried.

"Honey, we thought you had gotten married," her father said, holding out his hands helplessly.

"We figured, despite what the letter said, that you'd gotten pregnant," B.D. teased.

"No we didn't," her mother said sharply. "We were concerned, though. Mr. Cravath has gone on home."

"Two hundred dollars an hour, and he'll probably bill us for a full eight-hour day, too," her father grumbled.

"What were you going to do if I had been married?" Chelsea asked.

There was a sudden silence. All eyes turned toward her, as if she'd broken out in laughter at a funeral.

"The plan was to . . . to have it annulled somehow," her father admitted.

"My plan was to take old Con outside and rough him up," B.D. added. "You know, big-brother type stuff."

"I have the definite feeling I missed something here," Grace said under her breath. "I thought we were going to have some fireworks."

"Um, Connor, I think I need to make some coffee," Chelsea said. "Would you help me?"

"It's not a problem if you want to talk behind our backs, Chelsea," B.D. said. "We talk about you all the time."

In the kitchen Chelsea slumped against the counter. Connor put his arms around her gently. "What is going on here?" she asked.

Connor shrugged. "They showed up out of

the blue. No warning whatsoever."

"I know that," Chelsea said impatiently. "But why is everything so . . . so nice? It's eerie."

Connor smirked. "I'll tell you, I thought they had me for sure. I thought the brief history of Connor Riordan, Irish illegal, was over." Then he grew more serious. "The truth was, I was sure it was over. You know, *us*."

Chelsea hugged him close. "I was scared to death all the way home." She felt tears well up in her eyes. Connor tilted her head back and kissed her tenderly.

"It turns out your folks are pretty nice." He grinned. "I tried something new. Whatever they asked, I told them the flat-out truth. Everything. The good, the bad, and the ugly."

"I can't believe you're still alive."

"Eventually I offered your dad a beer, and Alec said if no one minds, could he turn on his baseball game with the sound off," Connor explained. "Marta drops by and talks to your mom, who I think is about ready to make her an editor at her magazine. During the break between game one and game two, we all run down to The Claw and your dad buys us dinner. We come back, I blurt some more truth. They decide I'm not such a bad influence after all, and Alec gets pissed because I can legitimately tell him I've done a better job with my girl's parents than he did with his."

"What did you tell them about us?"

"That I loved you like life itself." His voice was low. "That the wedding was designed to protect my worthless arse. That even setting that aside, I hated to think of life without you. Hell, I couldn't stand two days without you, let alone the rest of my life."

Chelsea kissed Connor again, more deeply. "I missed you, too," she whispered. She smiled. "I guess we should make some coffee. That's what we said we were coming in here for."

"No, no. I'm all for this blunt, forthright thing now." Connor laughed. "We'll tell them we've been making out."

"There's something I'm not quite ready to be honest about," Chelsea said. "I wanted to talk to you about it first. Don't answer right now, okay?" She stared out the window at the moonlight glazing the lawn. "I've thought it over, long and hard," she said at last. "And the truth is, I do want to go to college in September. But the bigger truth is, I need you there with me."

As soon as she was sure everything was okay with Chelsea and her parents, Kate headed down to the boathouse. Under her shorts and T-shirt she was wearing a bathing suit. She and Justin often went swimming in the bay on hot nights, heading out to a sandbar where they lay together and looked up at the stars. It was a perfect place for long talks . . . and for other things as well.

As she crossed the lawn, she tried to sort through the feelings churning around inside her. There was anticipation, of course. She couldn't wait to hold Justin and to be held, to tell him all about her trip, to hear all about his. But something else hovered at the edge of her thoughts—the fear that their relationship had been changed forever by the few brief days they'd spent apart.

Light shone through the loft window, but the boathouse was quiet as she approached. She opened the door, which Justin never bothered to lock, but as she stepped inside, the emptiness was instantly obvious. The boat wasn't there. The slip was empty.

Justin had left the overhead light in the loft on.

She heard bare feet on the wooden floor behind her, and the creak of the door. She turned, hoping it was him.

"Alec," she said, unable to conceal her disappointment.

"I meant to tell you," Alec said, "but everyone up there was talking, and I was trying to watch the game . . ."

Kate felt her heart skip. "Where is he?"

Alec shrugged. "He isn't back yet."

"He was supposed to be back yesterday evening. This morning at the very latest," Kate said.

"I know, Kate, but look, sailboats can't have regular schedules. I mean, you have to rely on wind and tides and whatever."

"Did he call?" Kate demanded, guessing the answer.

"No. At least not that we got, and either I or Connor or both of us has been home all day." He shifted awkwardly, as if he were going to take her hand for reassurance, then seemed to reconsider. "Don't sweat it. You know Justin."

Kate realized she was wringing her hands and shoved them down at her sides angrily. Damn it, if he knew he was going to be this late, he should have called. Of course, that was ridiculous, she realized. It wasn't like he had a phone. And she didn't have a shortwave radio.

"Are you okay?" Alec asked.

"Yes, I'm fine," Kate lied. She almost smiled at Alec's obvious relief. "But I think I'll sleep down here anyway, in case he shows up later on tonight. I want to be here to give him a hard time when he steps off the boat."

She walked back up to the house with Alec. Things had finally quieted down. Marta was on the couch, watching TV. Grace was out with David. The Lennoxes had gone to their hotel, but instead of seeming relieved, Chelsea and Connor were weirdly distracted. Of course, Kate thought, why shouldn't they be, under the circumstances?

She took a shower, then pretended to watch TV with Alec and Marta. She tried to relax, but it was impossible. She couldn't stop worrying about Justin.

She left the house with false reassurances ringing in her ears and went down toward the dock. The bay was calm and quiet. The sky was filled with high, thin clouds that shone silvery gray in the half-moon's light. The frogs were in a quiet mood, with only the occasional rude belch to interrupt the lulling, regular slap of water against wood.

The peaceful night was slightly calming, but Justin was on the ocean, not on this little bay. The ocean that could turn deadly in an instant, with no regard whatsoever for the life of one arrogant land animal on a sliver of wood.

If only she had gone with him. Then she would know for sure, one way or the other.

Suddenly, horribly, another thought hit her. *What if he had needed her help?* Maybe he'd suffered some calamity because he was out there alone. He could have fallen overboard without his safety line, the boat propelled away on the wind, leaving him alone and too far from shore to swim to safety.

What if, by refusing to go with him, she had left him to die?

Guilt welled up in her. When she'd been pinned down by the hurricane, storm-ravaged, drenched, alone, he had found her and rescued her.

And then, when it had been her turn to return the favor? She'd stubbornly refused to go with him and driven away on her own.

Kate tore her eyes away from the water and bolted for the boathouse door. She climbed the stairs and crawled into his bed. *Their* bed. She pulled the covers up around her.

Images were flooding back, feelings she'd never quite suppressed. She could still remember Juliana's eyes, sad and distant. She'd asked Kate if she wanted to hang out with her big sister. Kate had thought Juliana was only being nice, offering to spend some time with her dorky little sister. She hadn't wanted to burden Juliana with her presence. After all, Juliana always had something cool to do. She had cute boyfriends and lots of girlfriends. Whereas Kate was still a gawky kid with string-bean legs who was embarrassed to change clothes before gym class because she still looked so much like a little girl.

Kate loved and admired her big sister and had wondered for the longest time if she would ever, ever in a million years grow up as beautiful and sophisticated, whether her hair would ever look as silky, or her skin as clear. One thing was certain—she would never, not in this lifetime, have actual breasts.

And because Kate had been sure Juliana was only being sweet, on that particular day she'd said no. She'd said it shyly, pleased that Juliana had made the offer. Then she'd gone off to meet Chelsea at the library.

That night she found Juliana.

And ever since that night, Kate had asked herself a thousand times whether a simple yes might have kept Juliana from reaching for those pills. No, no, no, Chelsea had told her. Don't be stupid and blame yourself.

But when Kate had told her mother the story, her mother had stared at her, her own eyes reflecting and magnifying Kate's self-doubt.

She had failed Juliana, she was sure of that much. If not that day, then in many other ways. There had to have been things she could have done. Somehow, if she had only been able to understand what was really going on behind her sister's cool exterior, she might have saved Juliana.

"Please be all right, Justin, please," she whispered.

They were the same words she had whispered while holding Juliana's cold, stiffening hand.

EIGHTEEN

After staring at the blue numbers on his clock for what seemed like an eternity, Connor finally fell asleep at twelve fifteen. At two thirteen he was staring at the numbers again. He woke a second time at three forty-two. A third time at four ten. The fourth time he woke, it was almost five and he decided to give up on getting any sleep that night.

He climbed out of bed and rubbed his eyes with his knuckles. Nothing like working all day in the hot sun on virtually no sleep, he thought darkly.

He got up and took a shower. The shower pipes ran past Grace's room downstairs, but chances were she was staying over at David's. It wouldn't disturb anyone else, and at least by getting up this early he'd grabbed the bathroom before Alec could.

Somewhere between lather and rinse he realized what he had to do. He had two clear directions open before him. One involved total self-sacrifice. The other involved getting everything he wanted.

If he were an absolutely honorable man, he would probably go for the first option—walk away. No marriage, no green card, no certainty of being able to stay in the country he was beginning to love, no prospect of a life with the woman he knew he loved. It would be painful, but it would be decent. It would mean no legal risk for Chelsea, no risking her future and career.

But, by the same token, going quite that honorable all at once was a little much. After all, a man couldn't change his character overnight, could he?

Connor dried off and dressed in the cleanest clothing he could find. Then he crept downstairs, skipping the step that squeaked, and let himself out the front door, heading, as he did most mornings when he went to work, toward the boardwalk.

Except for a few obscenely eager joggers, the boardwalk was practically deserted. A drunk lay curled up in the recessed doorway of a video arcade, clutching an empty bottle. A pair of surfers were trying to survey the surf potential through fog that hung low and thick over the water. The sound of the waves, crashing almost silently, told the disappointing story.

Connor stopped off at O'Doul's O'Donuts. It was the first place he'd worked at in Ocean City, before some nosy immigration types had dictated his career shift to construction. He bought a cup of coffee and a muffin. He still couldn't stomach a doughnut after the time he'd spent frying and filling them by the thousands.

The lobby of the Ocean City Grand was empty, except for a newspaper delivery man wheeling in bundles of the *Wall Street Journal* and the *Ocean City Times-Gazette* on a dolly. Connor checked his watch. It would be best to wait. It was still not even six.

He had just made himself comfortable in one of the plush armchairs when a tall young man came through the lobby, wearing a blue and white United States Naval Academy T-shirt and matching gym shorts.

"Connor?" B.D. asked. "What are you doing here?"

He had caught Connor totally unprepared. What kind of nut got up to go running at six in the morning? Maybe someone like a Naval Academy midshipman.

"I was, uh . . . I woke up early," he explained lamely.

"So you thought you'd come down and eat a muffin in the lobby of the Ocean City Grand?" B.D. asked skeptically. "You do this often?"

"Actually, I need to speak to your folks."

"Without Chelsea being around," B.D. added. He made a face and glanced toward the elevator.

"They're probably awake out of sheer habit. At home they both commute an hour and a half to work every day. Actually, Dad commutes a little longer because he likes to drive kind of slow. Mom usually passes him in her car about halfway to the city."

"I don't want to barge in while they're taking showers," Connor said.

B.D. laughed. "You look to me like a man with a mission, mister. You sure you want to wait?" He stared at Connor thoughtfully, as if he were trying to come to a decision about him. "You going to try to marry my sister?"

"That depends," Connor evaded. "What do you think about it?"

"I think Chelsea's going to make up her own mind," B.D. said. "She likes to make people think she's all go-along and get-along, but she chooses her own way."

"I've noticed."

"Wait for them in the exercise room," B.D. said suddenly. "Mom makes the old man work out every morning. At least he'll be dressed by then."

"Thanks," Connor said.

B.D. started to trot toward the door, then turned around. "Hey," he asked, "Kate serious about this guy on the boat?"

"Serious, yes," Connor said thoughtfully. "What we're all waiting to see is how serious."

B.D. nodded and broke out in a grin. "She

used to have a crush on me when she was a kid. She seems to have grown up a bit lately." He gave a wave and headed out onto the boardwalk.

Connor got up and followed the signs for the exercise room. It was empty, so he lay down on the weight bench and closed his eyes to wait.

Kate sat up in the bed and looked over the loft railing. Logically, she knew that if the boat had returned, she would surely have heard it, but she was still disappointed when she saw the empty slip.

He still wasn't back. That single fact dominated her consciousness. Justin still wasn't back.

Her bathing suit and shorts were on the floor. She put on her suit, combed her fingers through her hair, and headed outside to the dock. Fog blew along the bay, shrouding the sun, but it was already beginning to evaporate. Justin could come sailing through that fog at any moment, suddenly appearing out of the mist.

Or not. She wished she could do something, anything. Kate glanced up toward the house, but there were no answers there. The answers were out on the water.

Kate considered swimming out into the bay. It would be a great surprise for Justin when he arrived to find her hailing him that way, letting him pull her aboard for the last half-mile of his voyage.

She heard the sound of running shoes on

blacktop and was surprised to see B.D. approaching. He waved at her and she waved back.

There was a time when B.D. Lennox was her absolute ideal of what a guy should be. She used to wish her sister and B.D. could get married, but they'd never shown any serious interest in each other.

"Hey, Kate," B.D. said, smiling easily and not in the least winded. He bent down to touch his toes several times.

"Hi, B.D."

As he stood, he looked at her quizzically. "I don't remember you being an early bird. Of course, I didn't used to be, either. But the Academy believes a midshipman should be able to get by on eight hours' sleep—a week."

"I woke up early," Kate said evasively. "I don't make a habit of it, though."

"That seems to be everybody's story this morning," he said. "What's up?"

Kate waved vaguely toward the receding fog hovering over the bay. "My friend Justin . . ." She smiled. "My *boy*friend Justin was supposed to get back yesterday morning at the latest."

"He's sailing, right?"

Kate nodded and bit her lip.

"Where'd he go?"

Kate shrugged uncertainly. "He said he was going up to Long Island at the farthest, depending, then heading back."

"And you're figuring he drowned, I suppose?" B.D. rolled his eyes. "Kate, you always have been a worrier. There was a thunderstorm the other day. He probably put in to port to wait for it to pass. Or else he decided to ride it out. Either way, that could easily account for a day's delay. Very easily."

"Do you think so?" Kate asked anxiously, searching his dark eyes for clues.

B.D. pretended to be insulted. "This is the U.S. Navy you're talking to here, young lady. Do I know about sailing? Does Orville Redenbacher know how to pop corn?"

Kate felt a fragile sense of relief. Of course B.D. was right. She was worrying for nothing.

"Poor Quinny," B.D. said softly. "Always worrying. I swear you were fifty years old when you were still fifteen. I think that's why you and Chels get along so well. You do all her worrying for her."

Kate laughed. No one had called her Quinny in a long time. But immediately she grew serious again. "He wanted me to go with him. I was thinking he might have been able to use some help." To her annoyance her voice had quavered at the end.

"Kate, when are you going to figure out that you aren't the one responsible for making the sun rise in the morning and set at night? Strange as it may seem, stuff happens that you have nothing to do with. This Justin guy is the captain of his boat, and if there's one thing they teach you in the Navy, it's that whatever happens on the ship, it's the captain's responsibility." He cocked an eyebrow at her. "It sure as hell isn't the responsibility of Quinny the landlubber."

"Don't call me Quinny in front of anyone from the house," Kate joked. "I'll never hear the end of it."

"Chelsea hasn't told them about that?"

"She hasn't called me that since . . ." Suddenly what little good humor Kate had been able to muster drained away. It was Juliana who had started calling her that, after she'd happened to see a first-grade paper of Kate's that contained a misspelling of their name.

B.D. nodded. "Sorry. I forgot. That was dumb of me."

"No, it's nothing," Kate said, hanging her head. She stared down at the boards of the dock and dug her toe between two of the slats. The fog was nearly evaporated, revealing the bay in all its early, sun-dappled glory.

"I guess I better get going," B.D. said awkwardly. "See you later?"

"Sure." Kate forced a smile for his benefit. But as he turned away, she called out to him. "B.D.?"

"Yes?"

"Do you know why Juliana did it?"

The question hung in the air between them.

B.D.'s expression froze. He stared at her for a long silence that seemed to have blocked out all sound, to have suspended life itself. He began to answer, then stopped, reconsidering.

"Maybe she was bored," B.D. said at last, his voice low and soft. "Maybe she was disappointed—I guess she'd been turned down by the college she wanted to go to. Maybe she was unhappy. I know she'd recently broken up with Steve Wasser. Maybe she didn't get along real well with your folks. Maybe she was getting into doing a little coke." He shook his head and made a face like he was tasting something unpleasant. "All those things were true. But I guess she killed herself for the same reasons everyone who commits suicide does it."

"What are you talking about?"

He shrugged. "Cowardice. Weakness. Self-pity. Stupidity."

Kate felt a flush rising to her cheeks. "Where the hell do you get off—"

"You asked," B.D. said. "I told you what I think is the truth. People don't kill themselves for good reasons, Kate. There is no good reason." He looked at her speculatively. "What would make you kill yourself, Kate?"

The question shocked her. She glared at him, furious.

"I'm serious, Kate. Say that boyfriend of yours never comes back, say he really did get himself drowned. You love him? Would you kill yourself if he died?" B.D. challenged.

Kate clenched her fists, ready to strike him, but he didn't back away.

Instead he came closer. "You know the answer—no, you wouldn't. *You* wouldn't do that." He smiled a ghostly smile. "You would never do it, not for any pain, not for any disappointment. Certainly not for the petty disappointments Juliana had experienced."

"You don't know," Kate accused. "Maybe she—"

"What? Maybe she what? What would make suicide an acceptable course of action?"

Kate unclenched her fists and took a step back. What? What *could* it have been? There had to be an answer.

"Think about it, Quinny," B.D. urged. "You know I'm right. You and your parents, you've spent years thinking *if only*. But it was never your fault. It was Juliana, and Juliana only." He smiled ever so slightly. "It's time for you to start looking ahead, Kate. Don't torture yourself because you have the strength and courage your sister didn't."

NINETEEN

By the time Chelsea got out of bed, Connor was gone from his room. He usually had to be at work by eight thirty, while she didn't need to arrive on the beach until ten, when the crowds started to arrive.

Kate and Grace weren't around either. And Alec, if he was in the house at all, was in his room and quiet. She got ready to go out, showering and dressing and putting on makeup. She always wore more makeup when she was around her mom. Her mother was a great believer in cosmetics, possibly because her magazine was financed in large part by cosmetics advertisers.

Chelsea headed for the boardwalk, filled with anticipation. She knew she should feel nervous, and she did, but it wasn't going to get in her way. She knew what she wanted. She was sure at last, and that certainty made her feel determined and invincible.

Maybe this is what Kate feels like all the time, Chelsea thought wryly. Probably so.

The boardwalk was starting to come fully alive. Shop owners were sliding back their safety gates, video arcades were beginning to emit their music of electronic beeps and bongs, the funnel-cake stands were heating up their vats of grease. The sea gulls were gathering by the surf line to squawk at each other and prepare for a day of dive-bombing trash bins and dumping on the heads of tourists. As always, the ocean went about its slow, patient business of adding a little sand here, taking a little away there, and gradually reshaping the continent.

Her parents were already at the table in the Ocean City Grand's restaurant, a casual place done in green floral chintz and blond wood. Her father was, as usual, reading his *Wall Street Journal* over french toast. Her mother was sipping tea and talking to him, unconcerned, Chelsea knew, that all she got in response were occasional grunts.

"Sweetheart!" her mother cried out, spotting her quickly.

"Morning," Chelsea said, bending down to kiss her mother's cheek. "So how is this place? You know, Grace works here." Chelsea took a chair and snagged a piece of bacon from her father's plate.

"It's not The Plaza," her father said, folding his paper. "But it's nice enough. The bed could have been firmer."

Chelsea shared a secret smile with her mother. Her dad would complain that a marble slab wasn't firm enough.

"Are you going to show us around town?" her mother asked brightly.

"That sounds like fun," Chelsea said. She took a deep breath. There was no point in stalling. She was going to do this, and she was going to do it now. "First, though, I need to talk to you guys."

Her parents exchanged a meaningful look. "I'm all ears," her father said.

"Do you want some breakfast first?" her mother asked. "Some eggs Benedict?"

"No," Chelsea said quickly. "I want to marry Connor."

Her mother stared at her. "The eggs Benedict would be easier."

"I'm serious," Chelsea said, leaning forward. Part of her was saying things like *Are you nuts?* and *You can't blurt something like that without preparing them.* But a bigger part of her felt supercharged, as if she simply couldn't hold off a second longer. She had decided. She was sure.

"I don't doubt that you're serious," her father said. "Could you tell us why? Why do you want to marry Connor?"

Chelsea winced. These were such dorky-sounding things to have to say to your parents. "Well, I guess because I love him. I mean, definitely I love him." She held out her hands, palm up. "I know I'm only eighteen. And I know we haven't known each other all that long, but Mom, Dad, I *know*. I want to be with him forever."

Her father raised an eyebrow. "Forever, huh? That's a long time."

"Have you dealt with the fact that he's white?" her mother asked. "You can't be naive about these things. This is not a perfect world we live in, and your life has been pretty sheltered so far, Chelsea."

"We know that a lot of people will hate the fact that we're together," Chelsea said. "I realize it's sort of inconvenient that I happened to fall in love with a white guy, but I didn't really plan it, you know?"

"If you were to have children, they might never be fully accepted by either race," her mother persisted.

Chelsea nodded. "See, I know all the reasons why it's a stupid thing to do."

"At least we agree on that," her father said dryly. "It's a stupid thing to do. Chelsea, honey, you're so young. I know you think you're all grown up, but believe me, there really are one or two things you still don't know about the world."

Chelsea bit her lip. She felt her resolve begin to waver. But then she found her courage again. "Daddy, you're wrong if you think I'm sure of myself. I know I'm young. Believe me, I totally know that I'm just eighteen and if I get married to Connor there are all kinds of things that I haven't even dreamed of that could go wrong."

"Then why do it?" her father asked.

Chelsea sighed. It was in some ways a question that could not be answered. Then she remembered—they had read the letter. In it, she hadn't tried to hide the fact that their marriage had a lot to do with Connor's illegal status.

"Look," Chelsea explained, "if things were different, I mean if I could be sure that a year from now Connor would still be around, I would wait. I'd rather have the extra time to be sure we're right for each other, absolutely sure. But the truth is, he could disappear at any time." She thought about what she was saying for a moment. "And yes, I could follow him back to Ireland, but however hard things would be for us here, they'd be much, much harder there."

She could tell from the look in her father's eyes that her argument had hit home. He glanced at her mother.

"What if he's using you to get his green card?" her mother demanded bluntly.

"I believe he loves me," Chelsea said as confidently as she could.

"Does he realize that by marrying you he might be destroying your future? I mean, is *he* going to put you through college?"

"I know all that," Chelsea muttered. She felt incredibly weary all of a sudden. She was wrung out, fading fast in the face of their skepticism. And now her mother had unveiled their biggest challenge—they would not pay for her to go to college if she married Connor. "I guess the truth is, I'm willing to give up college . . ." Her voice trembled at the word. She had to pause to catch her breath and start over again. "I'm willing to give up college for a while, until I can swing it on my own. It's a sacrifice I'm willing to make."

Again her parents exchanged a look she wasn't supposed to see. Her mother rolled her eyes and controlled a wry smile that was trying to break out on her lips.

"Fortunately," her father said slowly, "Connor does not feel the same way."

"What do you mean?" Chelsea asked in confusion.

Her mother sighed dramatically. "He was waiting for us this morning in the exercise room. Snoring, actually, but after we woke him he delivered a little speech, the thrust of which was that he wanted to know whether marrying you would mean we'd cut you off."

"I told him it was a possibility," her father said. "To which he replied that if marriage meant you would not be able to go on to school, then there would be no marriage. He seemed a little giddy. I got the feeling self-sacrifice doesn't exactly come naturally to the boy."

"Anyway, he said if that was our decision, then he'd go tell you the marriage was off and that it was his idea entirely," her mother explained. "Very noble. At least twenty percent baloney, I'd guess, but still, I think in the end he'd rather take his chances and lose you than screw up your life."

"The long and short of it is, if you are absolutely determined to do this, and nothing we say can change your mind . . ." Her father shuddered slightly. "Then, since you'd do it without our permission anyway, we graciously grant our permission."

Chelsea was stunned. Of all the things she'd expected her parents to say—

"Big conditions!" Her mother stuck her manicured finger in Chelsea's face. "You finish school. You don't start having babies until you have your degree. In exchange, your father and I will make sure you two don't starve to death."

Chelsea erupted from her seat, knocking over a glass of water. She threw her arms around her mother's neck, then her father's, then both together. "You guys are the best!"

"And your father will pay for the wedding," Mrs. Lennox said joyously.

"Wait a minute," her father said, pulling back. "Was that part of the deal? I thought we were talking elopement."

＊　＊　＊

Kate waited for almost two hours before she
saw the little blue and white boat, sails full of the
gentle late-morning breeze. She had walked
along the bay shore to the drawbridge and
waited there alongside the old men who trailed
their fishing lines down into the water while they
smoked their pipes.

Something had made her want to wait away
from the house, away from friends and their
words of comfort. She wanted to cling to a simple
faith that Justin would come, and, all alone with
the silent old men and the indifferent rush of traffic, it was easier to be sure that nothing bad had
happened to him.

She saw the boat the instant it cleared the
inlet and knew it was Justin. He would reach the
bridge in a few minutes, and the first person he'd
see would be her. For some reason that seemed
important to Kate. She wanted to give him that
visible sign of her love and devotion. Soon he
might need that memory.

As the boat drew close, she could make him
out, sitting at the tiller. Mooch was asleep on the
deck, baking contentedly in the sun.

"Justin! Justin!" she cried.

He looked around in confusion, then found
her. He waved and she waved back, big sweeping arcs of her arm.

"Sorry I'm late. Come on down," Justin yelled.

He grinned at her, looking weathered and even more tan than usual. He sounded his klaxon for the bridge, but the bridge operator was waiting for a second boat behind Justin to get into position before raising the span.

Kate looked down at the water, no more than ten feet down and plenty deep. It was an easy dive. But she didn't want to jump. It would mean riding the last half mile or so with Justin on his boat.

She shook her head.

"Come on," he urged.

"I'll meet you back at the house," she yelled. And at that instant it was as if every veil of self-deception was rudely snatched away. She didn't want to be with him on his boat. His boat was the enemy. It stood between them.

And in that frozen instant she could tell by his face that he knew.

They stared at each other, a hundred feet and a million miles apart. His eyes tore her apart and she nearly cried out *No, wait, you don't understand.* But he did understand, and there was no point in lying and making it worse.

Kate hung her head and broke the link between them. The center spans of the drawbridge began to go up. "I'll see you back at the house," she yelled again, trying to paint a smile on her face.

But he wasn't looking at her anymore. Mooch had gotten to his feet and gone back to him, begging to be petted. Or maybe, in some way, he'd known at that moment that his master needed him.

Kate caught the nylon rope he tossed her and wrapped it around the piling. The sail was down, and the boat chugged sullenly beside the dock. Then the engine died and Justin jumped ashore with the stern line and tied it off.

Kate stood there, arms useless at her side, while he made the knot and dropped a protective bumper over the side. Mooch leaped to the dock and licked Kate's fingers.

At last Justin turned to her, his face impassive. "Hi," he said.

She held out her arms and he took her in his. They kissed, a long, deep kiss full of longing that brought tears to Kate's eyes.

"I was worried about you," she said when they parted.

"Sorry," he said with a trace of his usual cocky smile. "Had a little storm and it blew me way off course. Then I had to lay up for a while and catch some sleep."

"I'm glad you're back. How did everything go?"

He shrugged. "Better than I'd expected, really. She's definitely ready to go."

She winced at the trace of bitterness in his voice.

"How was New York?"

"Well, we dropped the baby back with Molly and her aunt and uncle."

Justin looked at her, his eyes suddenly angry. "That's not what I meant, Kate. You know what I meant."

Kate felt as if she were breathing underwater. Yes, of course she knew what he meant. He meant *Will you come with me, Kate? Will you take my dream as your own, Kate?* "That went fine too," she whispered.

"I see."

"I can't stand this," Kate cried suddenly.

"I hate it," Justin shouted. "You didn't even give me a chance. If you had only . . . if you'd . . . but you wouldn't, even at the end."

His voice was choked and Kate realized his eyes were full of tears. It was a pain like nothing she had ever felt, seeing him cry, and knowing that she was the cause. She looked away as he brushed angrily at his tears.

"Justin, I love you," she said. "You know I love you. But—"

"'Love you, *but—*'" he mimicked viciously.

"I need to live *my* life, Justin, not yours," Kate cried. "I know that in my soul. I know you understand because I know you love me. I know you understand," she repeated, sobs tearing at her words. "I know you love me."

For a long while they stood on the dock under a bright and cheerful sun, staring no farther than their own tears. After an eternity, Kate felt his hand on her arm. She flew to him, crushing herself against his chest, holding him with all her strength as if with her bare hands she could defy fate and keep him with her forever.

"I guess I do understand, Kate," he whispered. "And I do love you. I always will."

Her tears trickled down his bare chest, and his dampened her hair. But eventually the tears were gone, leaving behind a hollow feeling. And slowly she and Justin disengaged, letting the first distance, a distance measured in inches, come between them. A distance that Kate knew would grow and grow, until only distance remained.

TWENTY

Kate bent her head forward and let the water pound the back of her neck. She was using too much water. She was using all the hot water in the house. It wasn't fair to the others, but she didn't care. As long as she could stand there, her swollen red eyes closed, and let the water pour over her, maybe she wouldn't feel the pain.

It was as if she had torn away a part of her body. Like they said people felt when they'd lost a leg, like it was still somehow there.

The rift between them had come so quickly and with such surprising finality. It wasn't how she had expected it to be. She'd imagined there would be a gentle way to tell him. She'd imagined tears, yes, but not this physical pain, this awful sense of loss. She felt like she had when Juliana died. As if the world had stopped turning and every law of nature had been rewritten, every face had grown unfamiliar.

Somehow she'd believed they would find a way to a future where they could be reunited. Maybe somehow, in some unimaginable way, they still could. But no, Justin would never believe in her again. He felt abandoned. For him, it would mean echoes of the father who'd walked away and then returned ten years later, another man altogether.

And yet, the rational part of her mind pointed out, hadn't she known all along, deep down, that this was how it would end? Hadn't she really surmised that they were two people passing on the same road, but headed in completely opposite directions?

There was a knock at the bathroom door. "Hey, are you ever coming out?"

It was Chelsea. "Sorry," Kate answered. "I'll be right out."

She turned off the water and reached for a towel. Her arms felt weak as she dried herself mechanically. The face in the steamy mirror didn't look sad so much as lifeless and empty.

She slipped on a robe and stepped out into the tiny, neat bedroom she'd spent so little time in since moving to this house for the summer. To her surprise, Chelsea was seated on her bed, bouncing up and down slightly as if she were excited about something.

Kate forced a smile. "It's all yours."

Chelsea shook her head and kept bouncing. "Guess what?"

"I don't know."

"My mom and dad said yes and they're still going to pay for my college and they'll even help Connor get a job my mom said maybe she could find him something at her magazine," Chelsea blurted in a rush of enthusiasm.

"What?" Kate asked dully.

"We're getting married," Chelsea explained. "This time for real."

Kate stared at her. "But, Chels, what about school . . ."

"I told you, Kate. Weren't you listening?" Chelsea asked, bouncing even harder. "It's no problem. They said they figured I was going to do it anyway and after they realized Connor wasn't some dirtbag and got to know him, well, you know, they figured better to say yes and help out than say no and put a rift between us."

Kate shook her head, trying to get her exhausted mind around what Chelsea was telling her. "I . . . I don't know what to say," she said lamely as she sat down on the bed.

"Say you're happy for me," Chelsea said with a huge grin.

"Happy?"

Chelsea tilted her head and looked at her quizzically. "Are you okay? You seem like maybe you breathed too much steam." Suddenly her eyes went wide. "Brilliant, Chels," she said, slapping her palm on her forehead. "You're upset, aren't you? I mean, about us not being able to room together now? I'm really sorry, Kate, I was so excited about everything, I kind of forgot. But we'll think of something. Maybe you and me and Connor could all share a house together, like we do here."

"A house in Manhattan?" Kate managed a dry laugh. "I don't think so. But I'll work something out. I'm okay with all that, really I am. And I truly am happy for you, Chels. I mean, you're getting what you wanted. All of it. I'm happy for you. Very happy."

"So those are tears of joy?"

Kate wiped her eyes and tried to smile, but her lip quivered and the smile collapsed.

"Oh, Kate," Chelsea said gently. "This is about Justin, isn't it?" She put her arm around Kate and hugged her until Kate could stop the tears.

"How is he?" Chelsea asked glumly when Kate had finally stopped sobbing.

"I think he's pretty sad," Kate whispered. "How's Connor?"

Chelsea made a wry smile. "I think he's terrified."

Kate managed a chuckle and wiped at her tears again, using the belt of her robe. "How are you?"

"Happier than you are," Chelsea said, and Kate chuckled at that, too.

"Yeah," Kate agreed.

"You gotta live your life," Chelsea said.

"Somebody has to," Kate agreed. "So what's B.D. think of all this?"

Chelsea made a back-and-forth gesture with her hand. "He'd be happier if Connor was, say, a naval officer. But he thinks Connor's an upstanding guy. My folks think so too."

"Well, by the time they all recognize his true character, it'll be too late," Kate joked. "You'll be married."

"That's what I figured, too," Chelsea agreed.

Kate looked at Chelsea earnestly. "Chels, I need to know something. If it had meant you were going to lose out on college, lose your education, maybe lose your career, would you still have gone through with it?"

Chelsea grew serious and cast her gaze out the window at the shockingly blue sky. "I told my parents I would," she said. "At the same time, Connor told them he wouldn't, not if it meant me losing college."

"Were you telling the truth?"

"I'm pretty sure Connor was bluffing," Chelsea said. "You know Connor. But my parents bought it."

"But were you telling them the truth, Chels?" Kate pressed. Suddenly it seemed terribly important for her to know. "Would you have put aside your own dream for Connor?"

Chelsea looked away, hesitating. At last she

met Kate's eyes. "No, Kate, I wouldn't. I would have done exactly what you're doing."

Kate nodded. "Well," she said softly, "I'd better get dressed."

"And I have plans to make and so on. My mom and dad are waiting for me," Chelsea said brightly. She stood, patted Kate's shoulder softly, and left.

Kate stared after her. Good old Chelsea. Sweet, decent Chelsea. She never had learned how to lie very well.

Grace lay quietly on David's bed, idly running her hand over his chest. She kissed his shoulder, and he responded with a kiss to the top of her head.

"You hungry?" His voice resonated through his chest. Then, as if responding to his own suggestion, his stomach growled.

She ran her index finger over the rough cleft of his chin. "Starved. Do you have any food?"

He thought for a moment. "I have Grape Nuts. But no milk. Also, I have eggs. I could make us an omelet. A Grape Nuts omelet."

"We could go out to get something," she suggested.

"That would mean getting dressed," he said lazily.

"In New York we had room service."

"Were they dressed?"

"I had bagels and lox in your honor. But I didn't get to that deli you were telling me about."

"That's about the eighteenth time you've brought up New York since last night," David pointed out good-naturedly.

Grace sat up and turned to look at him. "I know. I kind of . . . I don't know, David, the trip got me to thinking. I mean, you know me, I was already restless. But somehow when I was there, it was like all these things I'd thought of and dreamed of seemed possible all of a sudden. Like all I have to do is decide to have them and I can."

"Of course you can," David agreed.

"How many states have you been in?" Grace asked suddenly.

"States?"

"You know, as in Alabama, Idaho, California."

He gave her a strange look. "Let me think. Hmm. Fifty."

She poked him in the ribs, eliciting a yelp of protest. "You've been in all fifty states? Even Hawaii?"

He nodded. "I was military for a while, don't forget. And my dad got transferred fairly often in his job. Plus, I bummed around on my own after high school."

"How many countries?" she pressed eagerly.

"Counting the U.S.? Well, Mexico and Canada, of course—"

"Oh, of course," Grace said sarcastically.

"France, Great Britain, Germany, Hungary, Spain, and Portugal, if Madeira counts for all of Portugal. Then, in the Far East, Japan and Korea. How many does that make?"

Grace slumped back on her pillow. "A lot more than me," she said. She chewed at a fingernail, something she never did.

"Oh, man, you've got it bad, don't you?" David said a little sadly.

"Got what?"

"Got what?" he mimicked. "Wanderlust. The hunger for the open road. The desperate need to wake up in the morning and see something new."

"Wanderlust," she repeated. "Sounds almost obscene, doesn't it?"

He laughed. "It's lust, all right. Once you've got it, it's definitely lust. And I don't know if there's any cure. I mean, I'm happy enough here in O.C., but the day will come . . ." He left the thought unfinished, but Grace understood.

"I've never been anywhere," she said. "I visited my dad in California once for a few days. And I went to New York. That's not a very big percentage of the planet, is it?"

He stroked her hair. "It is a big planet."

Suddenly she slipped her arm beneath his back and held him. "I love you, David. You are the best thing that's ever happened to me."

"I love you, too," David said softly. "But . . .

225

well, I don't know, Grace. For some people, love means possession. They put down their roots and build their homes and families, and the truth is, civilization wouldn't get very far without those people."

"But?"

"But that's never been me," David admitted.

Grace snuggled against his neck. "David, are you telling me it's okay if I want to go away?"

David sighed. "I'm telling you that if you leave you'll cut my heart out," he said sadly. "But I can't ask you to commit to a permanence I can't commit to myself. There's still a hell of a lot of the world I haven't seen either. I have a buddy who runs a bush airline in Central Africa. He's been after me to fly for him. I'm not ready for that yet, but the day will come again when I am."

"I don't want to leave you," Grace whispered.

"I know, Grace. But you will."

TWENTY-ONE

For the next week, it seemed to Kate that life at the house moved along with a surface sense of normalcy. Yes, it was true that she'd moved back into her own room. And it was true that Chelsea was often on the phone with her mother, working on wedding details. But aside from that, they all went to work and did their laundry and hung out, just like always.

Well, *almost* everyone went to work. At Chelsea's insistence, Connor agreed to quit his job. She couldn't tolerate the possibility that he might run into immigration agents at the very last minute. He grumbled about being a "kept man" and made a point of telling everyone that once they were married and in New York, he'd grab the first job he could find rather than spend any more time watching *Days of Our Lives*.

Marta came over often to see Alec, and, as

usual, they divided their time about equally between arguing and making up. Grace spent a lot of her time at David's and went flying with him almost every day after work. She said she would soon be ready to solo for the first time and take the little plane up on her own. Still, she seemed distracted and edgy to Kate, not her usual sultry, sardonic self.

And Justin . . . Justin worked on his boat feverishly, seldom appearing in the house. He had given notice to the Beach Patrol and arranged to enter the race to the Azores.

Kate still went down to the boathouse to see Justin every day after she got home from work. Sometimes they hugged, or even kissed. But as if by unspoken mutual agreement, they no longer made love. They were trying to make their relationship over and turn passion to friendship. Somehow they hoped that might leave them each a part of the other to hold on to.

One day, as Kate left Safe Seas, she saw Grace waiting in the parking lot, leaning against her royal-blue Miata. Her uniform lay crumpled in the passenger seat and she wore frayed denim shorts and a white blouse tied at her midriff. Kate grinned and shook her head ruefully. It must be nice, she thought, to be able to appear so effortlessly elegant in everything from evening gowns to blue jeans. Whatever Grace's internal demons, they never seemed to leave a mark on her. Well, maybe a tinge of sadness in her almond eyes.

"Hi, Kate," Grace said.

"What are you doing here?"

Grace smiled mysteriously. "I need you to do something for me. I want you to follow me in your car. I'm selling my Miata."

"Selling your car?" Kate asked in surprise. Grace loved her little convertible.

Grace gave her a nonchalant look and offered no further explanation. "It won't take long."

Kate went to her own car and started it up. She fell in behind Grace as they drove from Safe Seas to the very northern edge of Ocean City, where condos gave way to homes on stilts and wide expanses of dune grass.

Kate pulled up to a cedar-sided gray house that rested on stilts perilously close to the ocean's edge. As they parked, a young man came out of the house and sauntered toward them. The entire matter took only a few minutes. Grace signed the title, resting it on the hood of her car, and the man gave her a cashier's check and shook her hand. Grace dropped her keys into his palm and, with a wistful pat on the car's trunk, said, "Take good care of her, all right?"

The man smiled kindly and nodded. Grace climbed in beside Kate. "Well, that's that," Grace said.

Kate pulled back toward the highway. "Home?"

"Let's drive for a while, if it's all right with you."

Kate pointed her car north again, widening the distance between them and Ocean City. Already the light was declining as the sun crashed toward the western horizon. In the brief glimpses between dunes, Kate could see that the sea had grown gray, as it did at twilight. For a while they drove in silence.

"I have something to ask you, Kate," Grace said at last.

"You want to sell *my* car now?"

Grace smiled. "Kate, I really enjoyed our road trip. You know, New York. It sort of opened up a lot of possibilities for me."

Kate nodded. *And closed off some possibilities for me*, she thought sadly.

"I'm not ready to go to school yet," Grace went on. "The truth is, I've missed this semester regardless. My mom's cut me off and there's no way I could arrange financial aid and loans and all that in the little time left."

"Maybe next semester," Kate said reassuringly.

"Eventually," Grace said. "Definitely. But I guess so much has happened to me this summer that it's simply wiped away all my plans." She grinned. "Not that I exactly had plans beyond some vague notion of someday doing something or other."

"So you'd be an undeclared major," Kate said. She expected Grace to laugh, but instead she was staring at Kate, studying her closely.

"You know, I basically couldn't stand you when we first met," Grace said.

"The feeling was mutual."

"And now, in all honesty, I can't believe what I'm about to do. In the good old days, I'd have done it and to hell with you and everyone else."

"What are you talking about, Grace?"

Grace sighed heavily. "Kate, I want to go with Justin."

Kate knew she should feel shocked, angry, even furious. That's what she'd have felt a week earlier. But somehow, for some reason, she wasn't entirely surprised by Grace's words.

"I haven't asked Justin yet," Grace continued. "Maybe he'll veto the idea, but Kate, I . . ." Suddenly she lost command of her voice. It cracked and she tossed her head in angry impatience. "Kate, I really want to do this. My mom and I— well, that's over. I can't stay in O.C., summer's nearly ended, and the idea of living out another winter here, working at some empty hotel . . . I have nowhere else to go, Kate. Nothing else to do."

"How about David?"

"I love David," Grace said simply. "I'll love him forever. But he understands. We both hope we'll be together again someday. I need him, and I guess he needs me too, in his own way. But I also have to live some more of my own life." She allowed herself a small, sad smile. "I know you understand that."

"That's why you sold your car, isn't it?"

"Enough money to pay my own way with Justin."

"It would be enough to pay for a semester of college," Kate pointed out.

Grace closed, then opened her eyes, a sign of acknowledgment. "I suppose it would be. But like I said, I'm not up for that—not yet."

Kate pulled the car over to the side of the road and parked it in a spot where she could see between the dunes. Waves were crashing on the deserted beach. Perfectly good waves, going to waste for lack of surfers.

"Are you still in love with Justin?" she asked.

Grace met her eyes. "Love him? Yes, of course I do. He's been my friend for a long time, my first true love. But *in love*? No, Kate. That feeling is only for David. And with Justin, it's only for you."

Suddenly it was too much for Kate. The tears came unexpectedly and there were too many to be hidden from Grace. "Will you . . . will you take good care of him?" she whispered.

Grace reached across the seat and took Kate's hand. She squeezed it tightly. "Someday he'll get tired of sailing around the world. And then, maybe, who knows? Maybe fate, if there is such a thing as fate, will bring you two back together. Until then, I'll try to keep him safe for you."

Grace asked Kate to drop her off at her

232

mother's condo on their way back to Ocean City. Kate volunteered to wait, but Grace declined.

It had been more than a month since Grace had been inside the building, and already the lobby and elevator and hallway that had once seemed to symbolize the limits of her world had grown unfamiliar.

She rode the elevator to the fourteenth floor, uncertain of what to expect. Her mother might be drunk or sober, icily cool or overtly hostile. That had been part of growing up with Ellen Caywood—the never knowing.

She had given back her key, and in any event she wouldn't have used it. This wasn't her home any longer. She knocked sharply and waited.

Her little brother Bo opened the door. "Hey, Gracie," he said, a slow smile spreading on his face. He glanced over his shoulder and made a face. "You sure you want to be here? She's—"

Grace held up her hand. "I don't care how she is, Bo," she said calmly.

He cocked his head and looked at her skeptically. "Come on in. Although I'm not sure I'm supposed to let you in without a passport."

Grace stepped into the luxurious and spacious penthouse. Her mother had changed some of the furniture since Grace had last seen it. The cream-colored couch had given way to a dusty rose that matched new curtains.

"I'll tell her," Bo volunteered.

"Bo," Grace said, stopping him. "How are you?"

"I'm fine, Gracie. Two more years and I'm out of here too." He grinned. "Besides, I spend most of my time over at Allie's house."

"Allie? As in, a *girl*?"

"As in *the* girl," he said. He sauntered down the hallway toward her mother's room.

Grace turned and looked out of the windows that wrapped around the condo on three sides. The one great thing about living here had been the unobstructed view of Ocean City, the ocean, and the bay.

Behind her there was a rustle. Her mother's first words would tell Grace all she needed to know.

"So. You back here for money?"

Drunk, Grace knew. Not falling down and undignified drunk, just that cruel, contemptuous drunk she knew so well. She turned to face her mother. Ellen was elegantly dressed in a pale yellow crepe pantsuit. A string of pearls and a glass of scotch completed the ensemble.

"No. I don't want money."

"Well, you must want something." She smirked. "You in some kind of trouble?"

Grace actually managed to smile. "No trouble, either. Sorry to disappoint you."

Her mother fixed her with a blurred stare. "I heard you're going to A.A. I have my sources, you know. I hear most of what goes on in this town. You weeping to those prigs about how rotten your mother was to you?"

"No, Mother. I go there because I'm an alcoholic. Like you."

"Speak for yourself," her mother said, waving a hand dismissively. "I don't think I'm doing so badly. You're the one here begging for money."

"I already told you I wasn't here for that," Grace said. "But then, I know how hard it is to keep track of details when you're drunk."

Grace saw Bo staring at her with surprise. Not that Bo hadn't seen them fight, of course. He'd just never seen Grace stay so calm. The truth was, it surprised even her.

"I'm leaving Ocean City," Grace announced. "I don't know when I'll be coming back, but it won't be for a long time."

"Not to college," Ellen said maliciously.

Grace smiled. "To Europe, actually."

Bo's jaw dropped. "Excuse me?"

"I'm sailing with Justin."

Bo grinned. "I always said it wasn't over between you two."

"It's not like that, Bo," Grace said.

Her mother snorted derisively. "If he's the captain, what are you? First bimbo?"

Grace sighed. "Mother, you don't reach me with barbs like that anymore. I've outgrown you. Like I've outgrown this town and, as corny as it sounds, outgrown the person I used to be. I'm past you, Mother. I'm past your self-pity and your weakness. You did your damnedest to screw me up and you very nearly succeeded."

"You think you're better than me?" her mother asked. "Of course you do, you always did. What else is new? You're all flushed with the self-righteous thrill of getting off the booze, big deal. Who cares? Not me. You're still a nothing, Grace, unfortunately, although I tried like any good mother. You think I don't understand you? Racy Gracie? Think I never heard that nickname? Think I don't know what it means?" She curled her lip. "Who do you think you are?"

Grace looked at her, at the fury in her clouded eyes. Their life together wouldn't end in forgiveness or acceptance. It would be, to the very last minute, what it had always been.

Grace took Bo's hand and squeezed it. Then she held him close and hugged him with all her might. "You're a hell of a cool little brother," she said, ruffling his hair with her hand.

She turned toward the door and heard Bo's voice, choked with emotion. "I love you, Gracie."

"I love you too, Bo."

"Oh, please," Ellen cried. "Cut the crap. You're not going anywhere. I'll see you a week from now, waiting tables in some south-end dive. Get out of here before you make me sick. Who do you think you are?"

Grace paused with her hand on the door-knob. She had known it would come to this, since the moment she had faced down Petie and realized there was still a much greater fear in her life.

She was cutting herself off from all she had known. From her home, from her mother, from the comfort she had found for a while inside a bottle. Who did she think she was? No longer who she had been, and yet . . .

She turned back toward her mother. And to her surprise, Grace realized she was content. She had survived.

"Who am I?" Grace asked softly. "I'm Grace Caywood." She winked at Bo and smiled her self-mocking smile. "The one, the only."

TWENTY-TWO

"Dum, dum, da-dum. Dum, dum, da-dum," Grace sang.

Chelsea shot her an anxious look and tugged for the hundredth time at the white lace veil that seemed determined to fall down across her face. They were waiting in the same small room in the same church where Chelsea had already marched down the aisle once before. "Grace," she asked, "why does the wedding march sound like a funeral dirge when you hum it?"

"Well . . ." Kate said, letting the implication hang in the air.

"I wasn't humming, actually," Grace said. "Those are the actual lyrics—dumb, dumb, dumb-dumb. Draw your own conclusion."

"I'm dumb?" Chelsea teased. "At least I'm wearing an attractive white lace number. You two are the ones in periwinkle chiffon."

"And matching shoes," Kate grumbled. "I certainly want to thank you, Chels, for making sure your bridesmaids look like dweebs from the 'fifties."

"Hey, that's half the fun of a wedding," Chelsea said.

"And what's the other half?" Kate asked.

"She'll find that out tonight," Grace said with a leer.

"You'll finally be legal," Kate said, helping Chelsea adjust the veil. "Not that you're thinking about your honeymoon at a time like this."

"I wouldn't," Grace said. "Might make her nervous."

"After what happened last time I tried to get married?" Chelsea laughed. "Nothing could make me nervous. Been there, done it, got it down pat."

"Whatever you say," Kate agreed. "Only . . . you know, I hope Connor's not one of those men who . . . No, we'd better not go into that."

"Shhh," Grace said sharply, holding a finger to her lips. "Don't scare her, Kate. Only a small percentage of guys are . . . you know."

"You guys are teasing me again," Chelsea said, trying to sound confident. "You are, aren't you?"

Kate shrugged and winked at Grace. "No point in telling her. Let her be surprised."

"You're teasing me because you have to wear periwinkle shoes," Chelsea said, looking from one to the other. "I mean—"

The door opened and Father Tom stuck his head in. "We're almost ready to start," he said, smiling at Chelsea. "You all look wonderful."

"You look good yourself, Father," Grace said. "In a celibate sort of way."

The priest flushed a little and looked down at the carpet. "By the way, we're not expecting any more surprises, are we?"

The three of them looked at each other and burst out laughing.

"I'm praying that means no."

"So's she," Grace said, pointing to Chelsea.

"You know, it's not too late for me to make one of you walk ahead and strew my path with rose petals," Chelsea warned.

Suddenly the organ started playing more loudly. "Oh, no, that's it, isn't it?" Chelsea groaned.

"Yeah, and the lyrics are still dumb-dumb," Grace said. "But good luck anyway."

Chelsea's father joined them, looking very handsome and solemn in his black tuxedo. He held out his arm for her to take, and it wasn't until she was close that she noticed the tears in his eyes.

"You look beautiful, absolutely beautiful," he said.

Kate and Grace picked up their bouquets. "Race you to the end," Kate challenged Grace.

"Oh look, the boys are all playing dress-up too," Grace said.

With Kate and Grace walking in measured strides before her, Chelsea and her father started down the aisle. Everyone stood as she appeared. Her mother wept openly in the front pew. B.D. stood next to her, looking bemused and terribly dashing in his dress uniform. Behind her family, she saw David and Marta and Grace's friend Beth. Chelsea's boss was there, too, and her co-workers. Some people grinned, some gave little thumbs-up signs. A few were fighting back maudlin tears.

In front of the altar, Justin and Alec stood side by side, smirking like bad boys who were being punished by having to wear tuxedos. Connor, wearing a black tuxedo and a bright, Irish green cummerbund, stood stiffly, as if he were preparing to die in some noble cause.

Strange, Chelsea thought. Last time she'd been sure it was really going to happen. This time it seemed unreal, as if there were no way she could actually be a married woman a few moments from now.

"Dearly beloved," Father Tom said.

Then again, maybe it really was going to happen.

This time, when Father Tom reached the part about whether anyone knew any reason why this couple should not be joined in holy matrimony, the only response was an audible giggle from several of the people there. Connor turned slightly and looked over his shoulder.

Chelsea caught Kate's eye. Kate smiled wistfully and shook her head. *No*, she was saying. *No reason.*

And then it was Chelsea's turn to say I do. The words came out a little squeaky, but they came out. And Connor started to say "Uh-huh," but caught himself and said that he did, too.

And then, quite suddenly it seemed to Chelsea, she was joined forever to a big Irish guy with laughing eyes, and a somewhat devious mind, and a good heart, and a poet's soul, and the smile of a mischievous little boy.

The next morning dawned crystal clear and bright. Kate could hear a breeze blowing past her window, a fresh wind blowing out of the south. Perfect weather for sailing. A perfect, perfect day for Justin to sail away.

She'd had the dream last night, only this time when she'd awakened, her pillow wasn't wet with tears. Whenever change came to her life, she'd had the dream about Juliana. But this time, while it had started out the same, the end had been different. This time, as she'd turned from that hopelessly still form on the bed, Kate had heard her sister's voice. "Good-bye, Quinny," the voice had said. "I won't be back again."

It was early still, but she knew he would be leaving with the tide, heading northeast to Nantucket, then away across the sea.

She dressed in shorts and a bathing-suit top. What did you wear to say good-bye to your first love? How did she want him to remember her? Did she want him to remember her at all?

By the time she walked down to the boat-house, he'd already brought the boat out and tied it to the dock, bow facing the house. Mooch, sensing the excitement, was running around like a crazed puppy. Grace was handing Justin last-minute supplies from the dock—fresh fruit and vegetables, and real milk that would later be replaced by powdered.

They were busy, the two of them, and Justin was down below as Kate stepped onto the dock. She opened the boathouse door and went inside. It was the same drafty, damp barn, and yet totally changed. Somehow Justin's presence was already fading away. She climbed the stairs to the loft and sat on the bare mattress.

It seemed like forever that she sat there, remembering. When he appeared at her side, she was surprised. She hadn't heard him call her name.

Justin sat down beside her and for a while shared her silence. Somehow his hand found hers, and the tears fell freely.

"I feel like hell," he said at last.

"Yeah."

"Was there ever any way it could have worked?" he asked, almost desperately.

Kate smiled bitterly. There was a painful lump at the back of her throat. "I think we both knew all along," she said in a low voice. "Maybe that's why it was so . . . so wonderful."

"It was wonderful." He threaded his strong fingers through hers. "Are you sorry? Do you wish we'd never happened?"

Kate bit her lip and shook her head. "No, Justin. I'll never, never be sorry."

"Wherever I go, wherever I am—" he began before his voice broke.

"I know," Kate whispered.

Chelsea and Connor were waiting out on the dock, holding hands and looking sleepy. Grace was wrapped in David's arms, exchanging her own whispered good-byes. Alec was pushing Marta in her wheelchair across the lawn.

Justin kept his eyes low and climbed aboard his boat.

At last, with many final touches, many sad looks, Grace pulled away from David. She started to climb into the boat, then stopped herself. She came over to Kate, a sad, wry smile on her lips.

"You okay?" Grace asked.

"I'll live."

"Of course you will. You're the Golden Girl."

"Yeah, that's me," Kate said.

"Kind of, uh, you know, make sure David's all right, will you?" Grace asked. "You guys could have him over for one of Chelsea's awful spaghetti dinners or something."

"No problem," Kate said. "And you too. You know. Maybe you could write me sometime. No, no, don't."

"I will," Grace assured her. She hesitated for a moment. "I'll miss you, Kate."

"Will you?" Kate asked, smiling. "Why? We're not friends, are we?"

"Absolutely not," Grace said. "But we've been the very best of enemies, haven't we?"

She turned and hopped aboard the boat. Mooch ran to the bow and barked. Justin cast off the lines and revved the engine till the boat began to sidle slowly from the dock.

He raised his hand and waved. Kate waved back. "Good-bye," she whispered. "I love you."

The current caught the boat and eased it toward the sea. As it turned away, Kate saw the final piece of work Justin had done. On the stern where it had always said *J's Boat*, it now said *Kate*.

The sail rose and caught the wind, and in minutes it was nothing but a small white triangle on the horizon.

Kate felt Chelsea's touch on her shoulder. "Man," Chelsea said in an awed voice. "Who knew when we cruised into this town at the beginning of summer that it was going to end with so much so totally changed?"

"He named the boat after me," Kate said. She nodded in satisfaction. "That's got to piss Grace off."

"Come on, let's go on a junk-food splurge, maybe go down to the boardwalk and spend all our money on cotton candy and caramel corn," Chelsea said. "We'll all go. Marta, Alec, David. I'll even let Connor come, as long as he doesn't look at any girls in bikinis."

"I'm a married man," Connor protested. "Those days are gone for me."

"Uh-huh," Alec said. "Guys always at least *look*."

"Oh, really?" Marta demanded. "And I suppose you think *we* don't?"

"Come on, Kate," Chelsea urged. "We have a lot of planning to do. The whole situation with dorms and apartments at school. We only have like a week to figure something out."

"I'll come with you," Kate said. "But I'm not wasting my money on junk food. I have to save up."

"Save for what?" Chelsea asked.

Kate smiled. "I just decided, Chels. Next summer I'm going to Europe." She cast a last look at the far-distant sail. "I hear you can meet great guys there."

Here's a sneak peek at Katherine Applegate's new series about falling in and out of love. . . .

BOYFRIENDS
GIRLFRIENDS

Look out for Book One,
      Zoey Fools Around
            —coming in February, 1994.

Zoey woke up late and hungry. The day before, she had worked straight through what should have been dinnertime.

She trudged toward the shower, scratching her head and trying to pry open her left eye. She brushed her teeth and started running the water in the shower. It always took a good minute for the hot water to come.

This time, however, it didn't come at all.

"Oh, man," she groaned through a foam of Crest. The hot-water heater must have gone out again, a regular occurrence. Either that, or Benjamin had taken one of his half-hour showers.

She rinsed and stomped barefoot down the stairs. "The damned hot water is out again," she yelled as she reached the kitchen.

"I'm sorry to hear that."

Zoey jumped, clapped a hand over her heart, and spun around. It was Lucas. Sitting in her kitchen.

Zoey glanced around in alarm. Her brother was nowhere to be seen. Neither was her mother.

Only Lucas, sipping a cup of coffee. A plate of sweet rolls was on the table.

"Your mom invited me to wait for you," Lucas said. "She had to catch the eleven ten ferry. Ben went with her. Something about school clothes."

"Oh, lord," Zoey muttered under her breath. She reached for her tangled mess of hair and tried to shove and pat it into something human-looking. But then she realized that, with her hands over her head, her Boston Bruins T-shirt rode perilously up toward her cotton panties. She slapped her arms down to her sides and tugged the shirt hem downward, which had the effect of drawing the fabric taut over her breasts. She released the hem and started on her hair again, then crossed her arms over her chest and tried her best to look nonchalant.

"You did invite me for breakfast," Lucas pointed out.

Zoey nodded. "Yes. Yes, of course, because I hoped you'd bring some of those delicious sweet rolls, and I see you did, so I guess I was right in inviting you . . . not that that was the only reason . . . I mean it's not like you're the baker or something, I mean I . . . we, I mean my mom and Benjamin . . . I also, you know . . . you know, we're like friends and all from before."

Nicely expressed, Zoey, she thought.

Lucas smiled his serious smile. "I guess I kind of surprised you."

"Why? Do I look terrible?" She cringed and took another stab at untangling the bird's nest on her head.

"No, you look wonderful."

"I don't think so," Zoey said, laughing wryly. "I mean, usually I try to wear something more than a T-shirt."

"Trust me, you look wonderful."

"Not that I'm wearing *just* a T-shirt," Zoey added quickly. "I mean, I'm wearing underwear." Instantly she felt the blush rising in her cheeks. She gulped and looked down at the table.

"Me too," Lucas said, grinning at her discomfort.

Zoey sighed. "I'm not exactly awake. When I'm awake I babble a little less. I still babble, but less."

"Want some coffee? There's still some in the pot your mom made."

"Normally, no, but since the hot water's out and I'm making a fool of myself, maybe I could use a cup. Or six."

Lucas got up and went to the kitchen counter and poured. She sat down at the table and reached for a sweet roll. With the first few sips of coffee, her confidence began to return. So she'd babbled, big deal. After all, it wasn't like Lucas had a lot of alternative conversational partners on the island.

This thought brought guilt with it. A mental picture of Jake formed in the air just over Lucas's head.

"Your mom can still cook," Zoey said.

"Yeah," Lucas agreed affectionately.

"Is she . . . are you two talking?"

Lucas shrugged. "My mom is trying to play it safe. She wants to make peace, but if she defies my father outright, well . . . You know my father, very 'old coun-

try.' He thinks he's the absolute ruler of the house, period, just like he is on the boat."

"Still, he's letting you live there," Zoey remarked, taking a bite of the roll.

"It's all a part of the same thing," Lucas said. "He's Portuguese, *Açoreano*."

"But isn't your mother from the Azores, too?"

"No. She emigrated from the Netherlands. The Dutch are a bit looser, I guess." He used his fingers to rake a strand of hair that had fallen over his eye. "That's where I got my blond hair," he said. "Just think Little Dutch Boy."

Zoey patted her own hair with her free hand. "Just think sparrow's nest."

Lucas appeared as if he were about to say something else, but he bit his lip and fell silent. The silence stretched awkwardly for a moment.

"Are you going to be going to school?" Zoey asked.

"Yeah. I still need a year, what with the youth authority being so much better at locking people up than it is at education. So, yeah, I'll be going to Weymouth High. I know everyone on the island will be thrilled to find that out."

Zoey nodded glumly and chewed the last bite of her roll thoughtfully. "I guess it will be kind of rough for you."

"And for anyone who befriends me," Lucas said, his voice dropping. "Which is why I want to say something. You've been very sweet, Zoey, but I don't expect you to talk to me in public. I understand how it is. I

promise it won't hurt my feelings if you blow me off."

Zoey hesitated. What was she going to do about this? It seemed awfully hypocritical to talk to Lucas here, even to enjoy talking to him, and then pretend that she couldn't stand him later.

Lucas grinned crookedly. It was meant to look tough and indifferent, but the corner of his mouth collapsed a little. "I'm a big boy," Lucas said. "I can handle it."

"No one can handle it," Zoey said. "You can't live life totally cut off."

Suddenly she stopped. She had reached for him without thinking. Her hand, dripping with sugar glaze from the roll, was covering his. Slowly Lucas's fingers entwined around hers. Neither of them was breathing. Zoey's heart was beating so loudly, she was sure he could hear it.

"I . . . I got you all sticky," Zoey said, her voice a squeaky gasp.

Lucas raised their locked hands to his lips. His eyes were nearly closed, his every movement in slow motion.

The doorbell rang. Zoey snatched her hand away. He withdrew his as well.

"The door," Zoey said breathlessly. "Probably Nina."

"I'll leave through the back," Lucas said.

"You don't have to—"

"Yes," he said regretfully, "I do." He turned away as the doorbell rang a second time. At the backdoor he paused, looking down at the knob. "Thanks," he said. And then he was gone.

☎
1 (800) I LUV BKS!

If you'd like to hear more about your
favorite young adult novels and writers . . .
OR
If you'd like to tell us what you thought
of this book or other books
you've recently read . . .

CALL US at 1(800) I LUV BKS
[1(800) 458-8257]
Monday to Friday, 9AM – 8PM EST

You'll hear a new message about books and
other interesting subjects each month.

**The call is free, but please get
your parents' permission first.**